THE
COMING
WILD HEARTS
NIGHT

Andrew Wichland

WILD HEARTS... STAND FIRM! WE FIGHT OR ELSE OUR WORLD IS LOST!

ANDREW WICHLAND

We shall never surrender

~ Winston Churchill

PROLOGUE

Just so we're on the same page, I might as well make this clear: even though I live on your Planet Earth and look human, I'm not. I am one of the last surviving free members of the Centaurien race of Centauries IV. To understand how I and the remaining free members of my people came to be on your planet, however, is to understand what happened to our people.

For almost ten years, I enjoyed a quiet life of peace on my Centauries IV as head of the planetary defense force, but war broke out across the stars—a war that threatened to engulf the entire known galaxy as we fought for the freedom of all known sentient beings—and perhaps more.

It all began when our allies, the Zorvains, stumbled across a planet we had never charted before. From the depths of this unfamiliar world rose a race neither we nor anyone else had ever encountered. At first, they seemed to be like most other races we knew; we never dreamed we could be so wrong. This race concealed their dark and deadly thirst to take over the universe, and when the Zorvains left the planet with an envoy, they brought something evil back with them that spread through the stars like a plague.

At the tip of their machines of war stood their most feared military leaders: Overlord Kizor and Supreme Lord Vatzor. It seemed there was nothing to stop them, but then came a ray of hope. The top scientists of the Centauriens, Paradines, surviving Zorvains, and other free people created a device that could turn the tide of the war: the Cybersuit. This was a vast improvement on the traditional Exo-Suit, a two-story mechanized walking tank with two legs on an armed, rotating torso.

I will never forget the day it was delivered.

CHAPTER 1

THE TEST

Because of my ongoing role as head of the planetary defense force, I was needed at the prototype test demonstration. The day it was scheduled, I spent the morning at home, reading a book about old Centaurien myths as I waited to leave. Halfway through a story, I glanced at the clock and realized I should head out, so I memorized my page number and closed the book's cover.

I went into the bedroom to put on my red and black dress uniform, and ten minutes later, my comm link alerted me to an incoming transmission.

"Answer," I commanded coming out fastening the last of the clips of what you might call the western bib of the long sleeved dress jacket with covering over the back of my hand. Which went down to my belted pants. On the right shoulder of my jack ornate cords wrapped under my arm. While medals ordained my left chest with a sash that went from my right shoulder to my left hip. As I check everything in a mirror it moved well with my six foot powerful lean frame.

As the link activated, a 3D holographic image of my second-in-command, Alan, appeared above it with his short crop of light hair and dark eyes.

"Sir, the test starts in an hour," he said.

"I'm well aware of that," I answered, adjusting one of the braided cords under my arm and then the medals on my uniform. "I'll be leaving shortly." I picked up my holo-tablet to review some files.

"Sir, may I speak freely?" he asked.

"Granted."

"Are you really going to go through with it?" I paused to look at him a neutral, and he continued, "Leaving the defense force for a combat Exo-Suit unit?"

Sighing, I faced the holo image. "I've stood by too long and let others do the fighting, but I can't do that anymore. I need to do my part in this war."

"But you are, sir," Alan insisted. "What is more important than the defense of our world—especially after what happened?"

Lowering my gaze, I thought of my entire family, who, save for my younger sister, Johanna, had been massacred in the civil war for my planet's freedom from a rival house or noble family. I looked up at Alan and nodded my agreement. "You're right: nothing is more important than the defense of our world. That's why I need to do this. I don't want to give them the chance to invade our world in the first place." I then turned off the tablet and walked out of my home with no idea that it would be for the last time.

The driver of the hover car and my aides saluted me before I climbed in. On the ride to the indoor testing arena, I just stared out at the world passing by me, and my mind drifted. I closed my eyes, remembering the conversation Johanna and I had a few weeks ago.

"Ian, we both know the war with the Wraiths will reach our world.

Whether we like it or not, it's inevitable," she had said as we ate dinner.

"But to activate the planetary self-destruct?" I'd demanded.

She'd looked at me with her deep, brown eyes, and the gravity of her determined expression temporarily shadowed her youth. "If the Wraiths move against us and our forces fall, they will modify our beautiful planet to become similar to their own. You know this. I see in your eyes that the stories the refugees tell pain you." After a pause, she added, "We owe it to our people and the generations to come to do what we can to preserve our planet.

We'll still be able to disarm the self-destruct function—the two of us are the only ones who can." The system required both of our retinal, DNA, and voice print passcodes; even if the Wraiths infested one of us, they would need the other sibling or the system would overload. *Before I could protest, she said, "Besides, the fleet knows what to do if the planet is taken or destroyed.*

You wrote the procedures after William invaded with..."

"They never found his body..."

She placed her hand over mine. "We can't dwell on that forever, Ian. What we do for our people here and now is what matters. Will you help me protect our planet?"

I looked at her for a long time before finally nodding. Hours later, the system was activated and the council was notified.

I pulled my thoughts back to the present and turned to my aide as the vehicle moved me closer to my destination. "Any word on when Shurgal and his escort are due to arrive?"

"No, sir," she said with a slight roll of her eyes and shake of her head. "After all, his escort doesn't even know when he's due to meet them."

Nodding, I returned my attention to my files. Considering Wraiths got information from people by possessing them, the need for secrecy was indeed vital. "Heck, Shurgal is the only person to even know the location of his lab."

We arrived at the test site, and as I climbed out, the man who opened my door saluted me. I returned the salute and slipped the tablet under my arm. "When is my sister due?"

"We just got word that her convoy is due shortly, Commander," the man said. I nodded.

People stopped to salute me as I walked past them into the facility. When I reached the main test area, I froze. Before me, with his what humans would call angel wings folded behind his humanoid back, a Paradine stood talking to two of the few Zorvain refugees who had taken sanctuary on our world.

"Shurgal?" I said in surprise, and the Paradine turned to face me.

The upper half of his face, like his muscular body, was covered in small feathers, and a black strip that jutted out emphasized his golden, raptorial eyes. Below his sharp nose was a set of full lips framed neatly by the feathers. Like me, he wore a uniform, but his was made in such a way that allowed his powerful wings free movement.

"What are..." I moved forward. "What better time for you to arrive than when nobody knows, and under no escort?" I shook his extended hand in greeting.

"Very true, old friend," he said, in a deep, raspy voice. "The fewer people who know about my movements, the better," he turned back to the Zorvains and added, "as I just explained to Ambassador Lizarda."

Nodding, I faced Lizarda, a tall, reptilian being with sharp teeth poking out from between thick lips and intense, glowing yellow eyes. In one of his four-clawed hands, each with ornate, metal bracers around the wrists, Lizarda held a staff topped by a sparkling crystal. His hooded cape shifted with the movements of his powerful tail as he moved toward them.

With an audible huff through his flaring nostrils, Lizarda growled, "And yet, Paradine, you would risk the safety of the very thing that could turn the tide of this war—and with it, the freedom of my people." He pounded the staff against the ground, and his scaly skin revealed a series of contortions from his bulging muscles.

"That is I why could not risk an escort," Shurgal said. "If my escort had been compromised by the Wraiths, they could have intercepted the transport and either destroyed or—worse still—seized the Cybersuit. All would have been lost."

"No one should question every precaution Shurgal takes," a strong feminine voice said. I at once turned and snapped to a salute.

With two heavily armed guards on either side of her, my sister, Duchess Johanna, came into the room, her ornate robe tied at the waist by a gilded belt. She was as tall as me, and her shoulder-length hair, the same shade of dirty-blonde as mine, framed her elegant face. Her slanted eyebrows, delicate nose, and full lips gave her a regal look.

As beautiful as she was, just like our mother before her, people often underestimated her commitment and ability as a soldier and duchess.

I knew, however, that she would lay her life down for her people in a heartbeat.

"At ease, Commander," she said, and I relaxed as she faced the reptilian. "As you have stated, Igonus, the fate of all free people lies in the survival of the Cybersuit. It should remain safe in our hands." Next, she turned to Shurgal. "It's good you made it here safely. Now let us all see what you've spent so much time working on."

Shurgal nodded.

"I'll go see if the pilot is ready," I offered. After Johanna dismissed me, I wandered through several halls and down two floors before entering one of the briefing rooms, where a soldier dressed in a form-fitting pilot suit stood alone. "Lieutenant Shazal," I said.

Spinning around, he snapped to attention. "Sir!"

I saluted back with a smile. "At ease, soldier. Excited to be making history?"

"Absolutely, sir," he said eagerly. "After today, this war will change—I can feel it."

Giving him an encouraging smile, I patted his shoulder. "Let's hope so, for the sake of all." His face suddenly twitched. I frowned slightly. "Are you okay, Lieutenant?"

"Yes, sir," he said with a nod. "Just eager to get out there to see what the Cybersuit can do."

Assured that he was okay and ready, I wished him luck and joined Johanna in the stands for the demonstration. Before us, in the middle of the indoor testing ground, a sealed pod was surrounded by various obstacles, a high wall, and a not-yet-activated force field that separated the stands from the ground. Shurgal stepped into the testing ground next to the pod, a mic attached to his chest.

"Ladies and gentleman, I welcome you to this demonstration. Today we see the dawn of hope, not only for freedom for those held in bondage but also for a first step toward peace throughout the known galaxy," he declared. Raising one hand, he pressed the remote in his hand; with a hiss, the pod began to open. "Before you is the prototype of the A-class Cybersuit!"

With bated breath, we all watched as the pod completely opened. Along with those in the stands, I got my first look at the Cybersuit, an armored suit in the shape of a lean, muscular man, its face nothing more than a blank slate of clear, featureless metal.

"Okay, I'm somewhat impressed," I said, leaning forward with my elbows on my knees, fingers interlocked.

"Let's hold judgment until we see what it can do," Johanna said.

"Now, let me introduce the pilot." Shurgal waved his hand, and a door in the wall opened. Lieutenant Shazal entered to a small round of applause and waved politely to the crowd.

With the sound of metal sliding on metal, the Cybersuit opened from the front like a cocoon. As Lieutenant Shazal backed in, the metal plates slid into place, encasing him inside. Before the face plate slid closed, however, Shazal's face contorted into a giant grin that made my hearts skip a beat.

Shurgal didn't seem to notice. "As a security measure, after it is first used by a pilot, each Cybersuit can be then used only by that pilot, identified through DNA encoding. It can be reprogrammed by codes known only by me, which I will pass on to high-ranking officials." Beside him, Shazal studied his encased hands as he flexed them open and closed. "We'll now test one of the main features of the A-class Cybersuit. Lieutenant Shazal, if you please."

Shazal turned to look at Shurgal, who pressed the remote again. With a flap of his wings, the Paladine took flight, landing in the stands next to me and Johanna. As he sat, the force field over the testing ground activated.

With a series of grinding noises, sections of the floor opened around Shazal. Mechanized reverse-legged drones emerged with rapid-fire laser and micro-missile weapon systems mounted on their rotating torsos. When the lifts came to a stop, the drones activated and faced Shazal.

Suddenly, the armor on Shazal's forearm shifted, and his hand was sucked into it.

Beside us, Shurgal continued to speak into the mic, "Through the use of extensive nano and bio-tech solutions, the A-class Cybersuit can alter your limbs, forming energy weapons called omega buster blasters," he explained.

Shazal, after eyeing the blaster, shot forward, firing pulsing shots. The drones opened fire on him, as well.

"As you can see, the A-class Cybersuit armor is capable of taking multiple rounds from the M-class drones."

Shazal absorbed some of the hits before taking cover behind one of the scattered wall obstacles. White the drones broke formation and circled around him from both sides.

"The omega buster blaster is capable of holding a thirty-second charge in the barrel that, when fired, can increase the weapon's damage capabilities exponentially."

The crowd watched as an insulated cylinder extended from the omega blaster and a light appeared at the end of the barrel. As the first drone turned toward him, the blast Shazal fired was three times the size and power of his previous shots. The explosion and subsequent impact twisted the drone, and it fell to the ground, a smoldering, smoking wreck.

As Shazal jumped over a drone zooming up behind him, I saw Shurgal and Johanna share a glance and a nod. Shurgal then turned to look at me. He frowned, switched off his mic, and remarked, "I can see from your expression that you still disapprove, old friend."

Slowly, I looked at him and Johanna. "Battlefields are the province of the living—not computerized machines," I said simply. They glanced at each other again, and I added, "War is supposed to be heartless, but without loss of life, it might well become a never-ending child's game."

They held my gaze for a few seconds, and then Johanna lowered hers and nodded. "I agree with you, Ian, but now that the Wraiths are able to possess our troops and learn all they know about our movements, strengths, and everything else a soldier knows, it's the lesser of two evils." She turned back to the demo.

Shazal was now astride one of the drones and circled, trying to find a clear shot.

"With the Cybersuits now being mass-produced, we just might be able to put our troops back on the battlefield," Johanna said.

As the drone twisted left and right, trying to throw Shazal off, the lieutenant aimed the omega blaster at the drone's top. With a wild swing from the drone, Shazal's forearm was forcibly shifted and the blaster transformed into an emitter from which an energy sword thrust out.

People around us started murmuring, and Shurgal switched his mic back on. "As you can see, the A-class Cybersuit is also capable of producing energy-melee weapons."

Swiftly, Shazal drove the blade through the head of the drone; it froze for a second before it toppled over like a fallen tree. Rolling free, the man in the Cybersuit charged the other drone. As it opened fire, Shazal cut the legs out from under the drone. It fell to the ground with a crash, the severed legs remaining where they stood. As it attempted to face him, Shazal drove the blade its head, as well, carving out a substantial chunk. Finally, the drone stopped moving and silence reigned.

The silence, however, didn't last long; the hangar doors opened and drone fighters shot out. Shazal turned, following their movements, and then dove out of the way as they charged him. The drones stopped and hovered before they turned back, and as he placed a hand on one of the weapon systems of the M-class drones,, the armor of the Cybersuit again began to shift. Shazal lifted one arm.

"We are now seeing the A-class Cybersuit's adaptive capabilities," said Shurgal. Curved micro-missiles popped up and soared into the aerial drones, which fell from the air, a bunch of fiery wrecks.

As the last one fell, I scratched my chin, deep in thought.

Shurgal, with a flap and *thunk* of his wings, took off into the sky as the force fields dropped, allowing him to land next to Shazal. "The A-class Cybersuit is capable of more than just reconfiguring itself to adapt weapons. It can also adapt to biological material, as well." Turning, the feathered man motioned for Shazal to touch him.

The crowd's murmurs grew louder as the Cybersuit reassembled itself into the form of a Paradine by growing wings and a face that were an exact copy of Shurgal's, right down to the feather pattern across the surface.

"The A-class Cybersuit also acquires a being's shape, size, appearance, and even abilities—like a Paradine's flight or a Zorvain's camouflage ability and bladed spikes."

The murmuring around us increased in both volume and frequency.

CHAPTER 2

INVASION

Later, Shurgal and I stood alone in the hall, and he faced me with a big smile. "Come on, old friend, I'm waiting," he said.

Chuckling, I shook my head. "Okay, I admit it: I'm very impressed. If that's just the prototype, though, I wonder what you have in mind when you perfect the systems."

"Actually—" Shurgal began but fell silent when my communicator went off.

"Sorry. I have to take this," I said, pulling it out of my pocket and activating it. "It's Alan." A holographic image of my second-in-command at the defense center appeared.

"Sir, we need you now. We've got something on the screen you should see.?"

I sighed and looked at Shurgal.

"Duty calls, so go," he waved his hand. "I'm not going anywhere. I'll meet you back at your place, and we can finish this discussion then."

With a reassuring nod, he turned and left.

"Ian?" Johanna approached. "You're leaving now? Shurgal is supposed to go over all the technical aspects."

I smiled. "I have a feeling he and I will go over everything from the armor plating to each individual nanite." I held up my communicator. "Alan just called me from HQ and needs me to see something."

For a second, Johanna frowned and lowered her gaze. "You should go," she said. When she looked up again, she added, "Even if it's just an undiscovered comet or an anomaly, it's better to be safe than sorry—especially with the Cybersuit now on the planet."

At once, I snapped her a salute. "Yes, ma'am." Outside the demonstration site, I got back into the hover car and drove myself to the defense network. When I arrived, the entire place was abuzz with activity; at the central hub, the most active area, Alan saluted and shook my hand.

"So what's the problem?" I asked.

He arched an eyebrow. "What, no hello? Just straight to business?"

I chuckled as we walked to a planetary satellite viewing screen. "Sorry, just habit."

He leaned on the satellite camera's holographic image. "Two hours ago, we detected several ships approaching the planet. They stopped at the edge of our defense network, but we can't get a clear image. We suspect they're Wraiths," he said.

I scanned the extremely fuzzy images of what looked like three or four ships and looked back at Alan. "Launch a heavy fighter, and let's see if we can sharpen this image."

Ten minutes later, the image came in clearer, revealing large cruiser ships shaped a bit like three-tentacled octopuses. They weren't the only ships up there, either; others, a fraction of the size of the large ships. The main superstructure appeared flat, like a big pair of wings. From this angle, I could just make out; the bridge in the middle was a small bulge.

Alan interrupted my thoughts. "Sir, are you seeing what I'm seeing?"

"Wraith Soul Command ships and Specter Gunships," I muttered. I pressed the commlink to speak with the pilot of our heavy fighter. "Yeah, we see it. Keep inside the defense satellite network, and do not fire unless fired upon."

"Yes, sir," the pilot responded.

I turned back to Alan. "Let's move to yel—"

"Sir, it's a trap!" the pilot shouted. "I have boggies decloaking in front and behind me! I'm taking fire! Repeat, I'm—"

The pilot's commlink went dead, and the radar screens suddenly revealed thousands of Banshee fighters.

"Red alert! Activate planetary defenses, launch all fighters! Get the o-Suit warriors to their suits!" I yelled. The last update I heard from the loudspeakers was that the Wraiths were getting through with mini¬mal losses. I jumped into my hover car and sped off to the Exo-Suit bay, where my squad was stationed.

I grabbed my gear and put it on as I ran into the bay. Karl, my head engineer, who was with me in the resistance and had been with my father before me, trotted alongside. As usual, his reliable presence reas¬sured me. My father had always said, "Give Karl a hundred tons of steel wool, and he'll knit you an Exo-Suit overnight."

Karl was a balding elderly man with a mostly gray, full beard. As he ran alongside me, he said, "Sir, I've outfitted your assault class the best I could in the short time I had. Some of the weapons are still not com¬pletely ready for use."

He seemed out of breath, and I chuckled. "Getting a bit slow there, Karl?"

As we stepped onto the lift that would take me to the cockpit, he shook his head. "No, I'm just getting too old for this, sir."

I shook my head as we ascended. "Never. I want you and Elise in the bunker, just in case, okay?"

After climbing in, I put on my helmet and initiated activation of the Exo-Suit, bringing the instruments humming to life. I looked up to see my squad mates starting their suits up, as well.

"Omega One, this is Omega Four. What are we up against?" said Terra, my fourth squad mate.

I sighed and adjusted my mic. "A Wraith task force. Last I knew, they were slipping past our defenses with minimal losses."

"How do they know how to get past our defenses?" asked Jules, sec¬ond-in-command of the squad. His head was bald, he had a mus¬tache above his upper lip and a small goatee under his lower lip, and he was what humans would describe as of African descent.

"Why invade us now?" asked Jen, my second squad mate known for her quick reflexes, with inquisitive, light-blue eyes that turned fiery when she fought. "Do you think it has anything to do with the Cybersuit?"

"Hey, maybe it's the scenery," said Casey, my third squad mate. He was a little shorter than I, with shorter hair and leaner muscles, but he looked like we could have been brothers. He'd been the sniper of the group until I became a better shot.

"Don't joke about this, Casey. This is serious. What's the status of our fighters?" asked Damon, my last squad mate, who had been under my sister's command in the revolution until he'd transferred under me. Damon was a big man with a lot of muscle, and dark hair and eyes. Initially, he had been one of my father's intelligence operatives and my sister's bodyguard, but he was still a very capable Exo-Suit pilot.

"Last I heard, they were dropping like flies," I said as we received the signal that we were ready to go.

I adjusted my Exo-Suit from crouching to rise to its full two-story height. I put it into gear and it took a few steps forward.

"Omega Squad, form up on me!" I said.

Quickly, my five squad mates raised their Exo-Suits, and we exited the bay. Just then, the curved-top Banshee fighters with stubby wings attached to the rest of the ship, dropped into view and separated, some heading for us.

My eyes opened wide, and I turned as far as I could in the cockpit chair of my exo-suit.

"Everybody, out of the hangar—now!" I shouted into my mic, but it was too late: the fighters fired into the Exo-Suit bay, which exploded right behind us. I turned back to the fighters still coming at us. "Get the track on those damn fighters and take 'em *out!*" I locked the missiles on my Exo-Suit, and after the pods popped open, I fired a barrage on our enemy.

The fighters exploded, and suddenly the sky was full of both Wraith Banshees and various Centaurien fighters. For hours, the battle for Centauries IV raged; for every Banshee fighter we destroyed, a swarm took its place. All too soon, my exo-suit lance and I were all that remained of our forces.

"Sir, I'm getting something on radar!" Terra called as I shot down a couple more fighters with a Gatling Gauss. I hit another with a pulse laser cannon before my eyes shifted to the radar readout on my helmet screen.

"I see it! Whatever it is, it's small and fast!" I said as I acquired a missile lock on more fighters. "Somebody get a visual!" I fired, blowing the fighters out of the sky.

"I have a visual!" Jen yelled.

Turning my Exo-Suit in her direction, I spotted the object flying in our direction. As I narrowed my eyes to zoom in, my face broke into a wide grin. "I think this demonstration is just getting started!"

Shazal, in the Cybersuit, rocketed toward us with broad flaps of its adapted Paradine wings. Below and behind him were swarms of M-class and aerial drones.

I watched as one of the Cybersuit's forearms became an omega blaster and a flowing energy sword ignited just above the other hand. After turning to aim, Shazal fired on a pair of Exo-Suit fighters.

"What the hell?" Jules suddenly exclaimed.

"Ian, we're taking fire! I'm down!" Terra shouted.

Surprised by the alarm in her voice, I looked over to see her Exo-Suit had fallen to the ground, its legs cut out from under her.

"What—" I quickly got my answer as the Cybersuit twisted in midair, its cannon charging and firing on Jules's Exo-Suit, sending it to the ground in a shower of sparks.

Casey and Jen turned their suits, and Shazal leaped forward. Casey fired his suit's plasma weapon, but Shazal deflected it so the blast hit Jen's suit, instead, knocking it to the ground. With a swipe of the energy sword, Shazal cut the arm off, and after hitting Casey's suit over the head with it, he threw it at Damon's, tearing his legs out from under him.

All the while, the drones fired not on the Wraith fighters above but on our forces, who were still fighting.

"Lieutenant, what the hell are you doing?" I demanded, establishing a commlink with Shazal.

Slowly, he turned to face me as he floated in midair, and through the link I could hear his sinister laugh. He then charged me, and one by one, the weapons mounted on my Exo-Suit were disabled.

For a second, I simply sat, stunned, in my Exo-Suit. A holographic face suddenly appeared above the emitter in front of me, and I eyed the wicked grin on Lieutenant Shazal's face. At once, I stiffened in realization. I had noticed the same grin on Shazal's face during the demonstration, but I hadn't made the connection.

"Wraith," I fumed with hatred.

Again Shazal laughed. "I thought you'd have figured it out sooner. I also thought you would have heard of me."

"Kizor!" I hissed. This was no ordinary Wraith; this was one of their most feared military leaders, Overlord Kizor.

"Who better than I to take possession of your acclaimed Cybersuit for my people?" He floated around me, flapping his wings. "Now, who is this lowly Centaurien on this barren battlefield?" His eyes narrowed. "It's none other than Commander Ian Erik Dregan. What an honor—you're a legend among the stars. Tell me, how many of our fighters did you destroy? Was it six or eight before the battle ended?"

I smiled grimly. "I counted around four hundred, Kizor."

He laughed. "The very last Centaurien fighting in this battle for your planet. Face it: you and your people have fought valiantly, but you have lost—and that guarantees my promotion. With your advanced technology, we will be unstoppable." Before I could speak, he continued. "Before I kill you, Centaurien, and ensure my victory, I promise you this: when we've taken your pitiful planet and added your people to our ranks, I will personally see to the capture of your dear sister. I will be sure to place one of my most faithful lieutenants in her mind, and I hope she'll resist, so I may have the pleasure of hearing her screams."

Anger boiled in me as I grasped a lever by my seat. "You better hope I die today; otherwise, you'll never be rid of me!" I shouted.

"We shall see, Commander!" he laughed again, and then his face vanished.

CHAPTER 3

THE ESCAPE

I looked up just as the Cybersuit lifted its charged omega cannon and fired. I pulled the lever beside me, and as my Exo-Suit exploded, my escape pod fired backward and landed hard on the ground, camouflaged by the wreckage. Kizor hovered above the smoldering Exo-Suit before he turned and left. When he was gone, I pulled myself from the wreckage, clutching in agony my broken arm.

I spun at the sound of footsteps and, when I saw my lance mates coming toward me, I sighed in relief that they had survived. Slowly, we made our way through the battlefield outside the capital.

Other survivors joined us, and we reached one of the nearby space hangars, where we flattened ourselves against the doors. Inside, Wraith-possessed Zorvain guards herded hordes of people into large groups.

"Oh, no," I murmured.

"What is it?" Casey asked.

I drew my head back to look at him. "They have Karl and Elise."

For the next few moments, we quietly debated our options, and then we formed into groups. I led a few soldiers to sniper positions, and after waiting for the right moment, we freed the prisoners. We then stole some Talon-class ships and a couple of freighters, which I was happy to discover were full of supplies, fighters, and Exo-Suits. As soon as we could, we took off, still under fire.

With my broken arm encased in a blue, liquid-filled cast and resting in a sling, I looked out the force field window at the disappearing ground, knowing it wouldn't be the same the next time I saw it. I closed my eyes, remembering the conversation Johanna and I'd had just a few short weeks ago.

With Banshee fighters hot on our tail, we'd made it into space. One of the women monitoring a sensor suddenly turned to me as we picked up a fighter escape pod. "Sir, we're picking up a Paradine ship escaping through Centaurien atmosphere!"

"Let's see it!" I ordered, and a holographic image of an almost avian starship appeared.

"Shurgal," I muttered as I took the seat in the center of the bridge. "Hail that ship right now!"

"I have comms, sir!" the man at the helm said, and Shurgal's face appeared in front of me.

"Ian, is that you?" he asked.

"In the flesh."

Our ship shook as it took fire.

"Sir, shields at sixty percent!" the woman at weapons reported.

I turned to the screen. "I don't think we have time to chat, old friend. Let's get to that slip gate and get the hell out of here!"

Shurgal nodded. "Agreed, Ian, but there's something you need to know."

Both ships shook as we took hits.

"Later! Let's move, people!" I said, and his transmission was cut off as we sped toward the large, metal ring orbiting Centauries' fourth moon.

"Sir, his shields are failing!" one of the helmsmen barked.

"Get behind him and provide cover!" I yelled.

"Sir, he keeps trying to hail us," the other said.

"Let him through as soon as we're out of this mess!" I said, sure that nothing could be so important that it couldn't wait until we were out of danger. I swiveled to look at another officer. "Activate the slip gate," she nodded, her fingers flying on the controls, "and then set it to blow as soon as we're through. We can't have them following us."

"Yes, sir!"

Just as Shurgal was about to make the jump through the gateway, he broke through to our ship's comms with another transmission. "Ian, one prototype! Eight operational!" His ship then vanished through the gateway.

I sat, frozen, in my seat, but was shaken out of my stupor as we took another hit. "All ahead full! Have the other ships follow our lead!" I ordered.

Our ships shot forward, making the jump into the slipstream just as a planetary laser locked on us; we made the jump just as the gateway exploded.

I pressed a button on my seat and strapped myself down. "All hands, brace for impact!"

No sooner had I said it than the ship shook violently again, and despite the safety straps, I was nearly thrown from my seat. Great torrents of white clouds burst from the overhead piping as the wave from the exploding gate raced toward us.

"Sir, it's gaining on us!" the woman at the science station barked over the clamor.

"Helm, ride the wave!" I called out. "Use its momentum to push us forward to safety—it's our only chance until we can reach an exit point!"

The seconds seemed to last for hours as the shaking got worse and the lights flickered.

"Sir, we're losing power!" said the man at the engineering station. "We have minor hull breaches—we're being torn apart!"

Alarms began to blare. "Radiation leak! All decks!"

"The rest of the ships are reporting the same!" the helmsman reported over the roar. "We're not going to make it!"

I bellowed to make myself heard over the noise, "Hold your course!" Just as the wave was about to hit the ships I ordered, "Exit now!"

With a great shudder and small explosions, the ships exited to normal space. As they shot forward, dancing fire spread in great circles from their exit points.

Inhaling deeply, I sat back in my seat, my eyes closed in relief. After a couple of seconds, I looked around and saw the officers at their stations exhaling deeply. They sagged in their seats, looking at each other, and then, all at once, a chorus of exhilaration rose.

My harness withdrew into the seat. "Damage report?" I asked, facing the engineering station.

"Fractures along the hull, along with minor breaches," said the woman at the helm. "The force fields are holding, though, and the radiation has dissipated. We're still losing power."

Those still celebrating became silent.

"Sir, injuries reported from all decks," the second helmsman reported.

I nodded. "Get medics there now, and have repair crews start at once. Get those fusion crystals working." I stood. "Once we're ready, we'll choose a destination and figure out our next move. With luck, we'll be able to rendezvous with the fleet."

"Sir," I turned toward the science officer, who was looking over the star charts, "something… something's off here," she said. "I just can't put my finger on it."

"Well, until you figure it out, the charts are yours."

When I learned the pilot we had picked up was a member of the house of Steiner, I almost threw him out of the nearest airlock, thinking he had betrayed us to the Wraiths. The matter was quickly resolved, however, when he said he'd been cut off from his family and then reminded me that we needed every man and woman we had.

When repairs were completed, the ships jumped into hyperspace. We were all silent, and I knew that, like me, the entire crew was reflecting on what had happened.

The people on board with a medical background attended to the wounded. After the radiation leak, most of the crew members experienced bouts of weakness for twenty-four hours, but then everyone seemed fine. Even so, the doctor who quickly took charge insisted on examining everyone.

"Doc, I feel great," I protested from a med bed as she readied an instrument. "I don't think I need another physical," I continued. "I already had one this year."

"Sorry, sir, no exceptions." Her long, dark hair matched her ebony skin; she pressed the instrument against my arm and, with a hiss, drew blood. "Frankly, I don't expect any differences from the hundreds of samples my staff and I have already taken." She slipped the vial into a scanner and rubbed her chin as the results came up. "Metabolism climbing, as well as muscle tone and energy." She turned to look at me as I slipped my shirt back on. "Saying you're fine is an understatement."

"Then I guess that radiation did us good," I said, slipping my shoes on.

"Not this good." The doctor pointed at the screen. "There should at least be some cellular-level damage."

Smiling, I climbed to my feet. "Well, I'm sure you'll find something—otherwise, you'd be out of a job."

Before she could reply, I heard pounding feet, and the science officer appeared at the door.

CHAPTER 4

THE LONG WAIT

"Sir, you need to see this!" she barked as she held up a holo-tablet.

I frowned at the urgency in her voice. "What is it?"

"Just look," she said, bringing it forward.

For a couple of seconds, I scowled at the stars floating above the screen before slowly lifting my gaze. "I enjoy looking at the stars as much as the next guy, but—"

"Sir," she interrupted, flicking her hand across the image. Immediately, the stars shifted. "This image was taken about three months ago from this area of space of the same stars." She flicked the image back to the first. "I took this one a few moments ago."

I glanced down at the image again before flipping between them, and then it hit me like a starship at slip speed. "That's impossible," I muttered. "Movement and the deaths and births of stars like this don't happen this fast..." Fear crept into my voice as I looked up at her. "It takes—"

"Centuries," she finished for me, "or millennia." She looked from me to the doctor. "By my calculations—and I went over them again and again—we're at least...."

"At least what?" I encouraged her, placing a hand on her shoulder.

She bit her lip and her eyes grew moist. "At least five-thousand years in the past," she finally said.

I was too stunned to speak.

Finally, the doctor said, "Are you sure, Lieutenant? "Maybe your calculations—"

"She's not wrong, Doc," I said, turning away. "Lieutenant, have you figured out a way to get us home?"

"That's just it, sir," she said, and I looked at her. "I don't think there is, unless you want to replicate the explosion of the slip gate—and nobody here is a slip gate expert."

I was silent for a second. "Doc," I turned to her, "is there any way we can build cryosleep pods?"

"Between me and Karl, it might be possible," she said, biting her lip, "but it would take decades with no guarantee that it would work or that the ships wouldn't still be in danger while we slept."

Again, silence fell.

"Tell no one of our situation," I finally said as they both looked at me. "I'll make a ship-wide announcement shortly, once we have a clearer idea of where to go and what to do."

I turned to face the doctor. "I want you to consult with Karl and figure out any options for getting back."

For the next couple of days, we continued making repairs. Doc attended the injured and completed further tests to determine the aftermath of our radiation exposure. Secretly, she worked with Karl to form a plan to keep us alive.

For nearly a week, we drifted in that section of space, and all the while I tried to think of a way to break the bad news to the crew.

One day, as I was just getting ready to gather everyone, Doc said, "Sir!" through my communicator.

Sighing, I put down my tablet and turned toward her holographic face. "I'm a little busy here."

"Then stop what you're doing and get down here—you have to see this!" she snapped.

Soon I stood again in the medical unit, looking at another holographic image. This one showed what appeared to be a cluster of free-ly-flowing cells.

"Okay, what am I looking at?" I asked, my arms crossed over my chest.

"That is a cellular sample I took of one of the more..." I glanced at her, "*mature* members of our group," she finally finished. "As you can see, the sample clearly shows signs of age." She then swiped the image. "Same cells, present time. See any difference?"

After glancing at her, I eyed the cells. "They seem... faster," I said finally.

"Not just that," Doc said, and I gave her my full attention. "There are also almost four times as many of them. In other words, this second sample is as if it came from someone almost half his age."

I frowned. "Is what you say... I mean, what you're saying is impossible! You're saying this guy aged... backward? He *reverse* aged?" I waved my hand at the image.

"Well, don't just take my word for it," Doc said. I turned as the door to the other room opened and then gaped as Karl, with a lot less gray in his hair and beard, fewer wrinkles, and a restored hairline, stepped into the room. The doctor said, "Because I've been with Karl for the past couple of days, I can tell you he hasn't received any cosmetics. Commander, the radiation affected us in the most impossible way. Instead of killing us, it's making some of us younger."

"And the rest?" I asked.

Sighing, she looked at me. "Those around our age are stabilizing. As for the children... for now, they're dormant," she explained, "but that could change when they reach maturity."

Later, I stood in the bridge of the ship, not sure I was ready to announce what I had to. "Lieutenant," I finally said, and the communications officer turned to me, "give me ship-wide access and also connect me to the other ships."

He must have noticed the hollow tone in my voice, because he frowned. "Whenever you're ready."

After taking a deep breath to steady myself, I announced, "Attention, all personnel. This is Commander Dregan. I must tell you some facts that have recently been revealed to me by a member of the crew. There is no easy way to say this." Feeling like I was about to jump out of an airlock, I continued, "When the ship exploded as we traveled through the slip gate, we didn't just travel light years away from our home. Somehow, we also traveled back through time," the people around me froze, "by about five thousand years. All the friends and family we left behind... they haven't been born yet. We have only one sure way of returning to them."

For a few seconds, silence reigned.

"Undoubtedly by now, you have noticed certain members of us have begun to experience changes. I've come to the realization that the radiation we were exposed to has affected us."

The bridge crew turned from their stations to look at me.

"Instead of harming us, the radiation appears to be regenerating us. The effect is most obvious in our elderly population," I explained, ignoring the murmurs of the crew around me. "In short, by a freak accident, we may very well have gained eternal youth. The path we now walk is long, and we will have to face countless trials, but we have only one goal: to survive and return to our home, which has been stolen from us.

"After spending the last few days poring over charts, I have decided on a planet on which we can hide. It was recently discovered by scouts who returned to Centauries shortly before the invasion. It's primitive, but its occupants physically resemble us perfectly. They call this planet Earth," I continued. "I ask you all to follow me to the unknown to wait, plan, and one day reclaim what was taken from us!" I cried out the last words, brandishing my fist in the air.

Even through the doors, I heard cheers reverberate from the speakers.

"One day, we will make the Wraiths pay for invading our world! One day, we will make them wish they had never risen from that dark planet that spawned them! We will rejoin Shurgal to claim the Cybersuits, we will have our vengeance, and our people will know freedom again!"

The cheers grew even louder when those around me stood and cheered.

"Helm," the woman faced me, "set the course and take us to hyperspace!"

"Yes, sir!" she cried with a salute.

When our scouts visited Planet Earth five-thousand years after our current predicament, the humans they had observed were not the same people we met now.

We quickly adapted and hid among their race, and as the years passed, we kept out of their history as much as we could. On the continent of North America, we built an underground base to house our entire population. We settled into peaceful days filled with learning and training, but I never forgot that, one day, I would face Overlord Kizor again.

When I got restless, I left the group and traveled Earth. I learned from the humans how to fight in various ways, each time under a new identity. Some identities started our newer technology, making me look younger through advanced cosmetics, and allowing me to be accepted into families. It was during one of these adventures that I learned that Casey was my half-brother and I fell in love.

Around the early 1990s, human time, and not long after the invasion of our world, Terra and I were married. When she vanished, I was devastated, but I looked for her for four years without finding a single trace.

Thirteen years later, as I was celebrating our anniversary at the base with the usual bottle of alcohol—this year a hundred-year-old scotch—and videos of us together, someone knocked on my door.

"Go away," I said, holding another full glass from the half-finished bottle as I watched our wedding video.

"Ian, it's me." The voice belonged to Jules.

"You know what day it is," I said through my door, draining the glass in one go.

"They're here, Ian," he said.

As I started to refill the glass, I dropped the bottle. It shattered on the floor, and the remaining liquor went everywhere, the stench of alcohol permeating the air. "What?" I demanded.

"The Wraiths are here," he said.

CHAPTER 5

THE DEEP BREATH
BEFORE THE PLUNGE

Alec

With the final period bell still ringing in my ears, I walked to my locker to put my things away. I barely heard the noise around me, preoccupied with the events of the day, as I spun the combination, unlocked the pad-lock, and set my books inside.

Someone tapped me on my shoulder, and I turned, frowning when I noticed the person next to me was still putting her things away. Turning the other way, I sighed at the sight of my friend, Hunter, and his ever-present grin. He was about my height, with short, light-brown hair and an athletic build just like mine.

"What is it, Hunter?" I asked, peering back into my locker.

"You're not still thinking about the hockey tryouts, are you?" he asked, shaking his head. "We can always try out again." I just shrugged. "Or maybe we can go for one of those," he nodded toward the wall behind me. Turning, I eyed the posters for two of the city's premier martial arts schools: Black Tiger and Golden Dragon. "Especially Golden Dragon, with their annual scholarship drawing," Hunter continued. "Who would say no to a year of free training?"

"Yeah, maybe," I said.

Golden Dragon Academy of Martial Arts had been operated by the same Japanese family for almost fifty years and had become so successful that new schools were popping up throughout the country. They had a reputation for caring about the people they trained, and every year they ran a scholarship lottery for a full-year of lessons.

Black Tiger had been established a few years ago by an organization called U.N.I.T.Y. whose two octagon interlocked by one corner logo graced the each poster. Their manifesto was to help kids stay off drugs and the streets. Black Tiger was one of several programs partnered by them in collaboration with several city and federal law enforcement agencies.

As I started to turn, I eyed a girl about my age, Aisha, down the hall in a T-shirt and jeans. She had a slim, petite build, emphasized by her clothing. Framing her ebony face was a hijab scarf, which was a light blue today, matching her electric eyes. She wore a messenger bag slung from one shoulder to her opposite hip. On one wrist was a plastic key ring slinky, and in her hand was her red-tipped white cane, which was folded up at the moment.

I often saw Aisha sitting alone on the bus, one ear with an ear¬phone and the one toward the aisle open, her head lightly bobbing to her music. From various conversations, I'd learned she had been born without her eyes but wore prosthetics so people would stop trying to look for the empty space behind her sunglasses.

Her friend, Blair, whose long, dark hair stretched down her backpack, was next to her. Blair's locker was lower than the others for easier access from her wheelchair. Two years earlier, she and her mother had been in a car accident while on their way to one of Blair's dance recit¬als. The winter weather had been terrible and the roads slippery, and her mother had lost control and crashed headlong into an eighteen-wheeler transporting benzene. The emergency crew had barely gotten Blair out before both truck and car exploded. The fire had burned for hours; by the time they had put it out, the only things that remained were twisted pieces of metal.

The pair were such close friends that I hardly ever saw them apart, and that had been true even before fate had put Blair in her chair. When people made fun of Aisha or harassed her in—or even outside of—school, Blair always fought for and defended her. I often heard that behind her model-like face was Wolverine without the claws.

"So, when are you going to just ask her out?"

I jerked back and stared daggers at Hunter, but he simply grinned back. "What are you talking about?" I demanded, slinging my bag over my shoulder as I turned to leave.

"Oh, come on, Alec," he followed me, "I've caught you making googly eyes at her since we were kids."

Before I could reply, I bumped into something—or, rather, someone. "Sorry!" I said, turning, before adding reflexively, "Hey, Gavin."

The teen's platinum blond hair stretched down to his shoulders, and like every day, all day, he wore a long coat that reached the heels of his boots. He paused and looked at me over his shoulder, which was curved by his partially-hunched back. As always, the intense look in his golden eyes sent a slight shiver down my spine. He turned silently and kept walking.

"Well, Captain Creepy sure knows how to make a mark," Hunter said as we watched Gavin stop at the lottery sign-up sheet and jot down his information. "Maybe we should go with the other one."

Shaking my head, I looked at Hunter. "Well, considering his dad abandoned him *and* his mother, what do you expect?" I countered. "He clearly has some kind of a spinal problem, and he's had to take care of his mother practically on his own. She has MS, you know."

Hunter shrugged. "The fact that they live in the woods outside of town doesn't scream Unabomber to you?"

"No," I answered. "The fact that, last week, I saw him stare down three bullies picking on a kid half their size says something completely different to me." I glanced quickly at my smartphone, but there were no messages.

"Hi, Alec." The soft voice rooted me to the spot. Biting my lips, I slowly turned to see Aisha right behind me, her head turned in my direction. Blair, who had led her over, parked beside her.

"Hey, Aisha," I answered, mentally kicking myself for not being able to think of something better.

"Having a good day so far?" she inquired.

"You could say that," I answered as Blair rolled her eyes at me. For a second, silence stretched between us.

"So…" Hunter said, breaking it, "are you two thinking of trying out for the scholarship draw?"

"I heard Golden Dragon has a great tai chi and forms program," Aisha sounded interested.

"Yeah, it might be cool," Blair nodded.

"Like the hotrod could even take anyone out," a voice laughed as two boys came down the hall.

At once, Blair's face hardened, and I caught a glint of steel in her eye. Gripping the rings on the wheels of her chair, she whipped around, ramming the footrests into one of the passing teen's shins. He yowled in pain and went sprawling to the floor.

"Oh, I am so sorry!" Blair said innocently, hands covering her mouth. "I'm still getting used to how much space I need to turn."

I rolled my eyes but froze when I saw who she had hit. It was hard not to recognize him, what with all the posters displayed in the school hallways of him posing to show off his bulging, toned muscles, boyish good looks, and short, dark hair. It was Bradley, star quarterback and Black Tiger student.

"Let's get out of here!" Hunter hissed, shifting away. "I don't want to catch any more heat from her."

"You stay right where you are!" a voice snapped.

Groaning, Hunter froze, and we all turned to look at Vice Principal Plumber, and his crony, Officer Anderson, waiting before us.

"What is going on here?" Plumber demanded, staring at us pointedly.

"She hit me!" Bradley accused, pointing at Blair.

"It was an accident," she said, turning her chair to face the vice principal.

"Like it was the last five times?" Plumber demanded, shooting her a look. "Somebody get him to the nurse's office!" he snapped, and a few teens came forward and helped Bradley hobble off, his arms slung over their shoulders.

"Sir, it was an accident," Aisha turned in the direction of his voice. "We were talking, and as Blair turned, Bradley walked right into her chair."

"Enough of that. Both of you are to report to my office for detention."

Blinking at the injustice, I stepped forward. "For what?" I demanded.

"That's not fair!" Hunter snapped.

"Don't you take that tone with me!" Plumber said sharply. "For Miss Blair, it's for attacking a fellow student. For Miss Aisha and you two," he pointed at me and Hunter, and we gasped, "it's for enabling her. Now, all of you go to my office before it gets worse."

Hunter and I spluttered at what he said, and then he walked away.

Ian

As the cleaning bots hovered out of their compartment to pick up the broken bottle, I dropped the glass and rushed toward the door, running my fingers through my hair. *Wraiths.* I grabbed my hip holsters, which held two blasters that looked like the human Glock, but with the barrel cut short and the blaster emitter and power mag in front of the trigger guard.

I pressed the release button and the door slid into the wall, finally revealing Jules. Together, we walked down the hall as I snapped on my gun belt and buckled the holsters to my thighs. As we began to jog, he stared at me with dark eyes, looking both worried and thoughtful.

"Ian, you can't keep doing this to yourself. Terra wouldn't—" he started.

"Who knows what she would want? She's been gone thirteen years, Jules," I said as we entered the command center.

It was flooded with activity and people ran from console to console, each displaying holographic images. Jules and I hurried to a manned console, which included the readings of one of our planetary sensor satellites. It showed two groups of ships speeding toward each other, while larger ships hung back.

As I got near the station, Jen, Casey, Klaus, Elise, and Damon arrived. Our years on Earth had hardly changed them, although Jen and Casey had been married for twenty years now. A few centuries back, Damon had shaved off his thick beard at the request of his wife.

Klaus once the pilot we picked up joined our group and was now commander of our fighter core. He was as tall and muscular as I was, and his light mustache and beard circled his mouth. He had acquired a light German accent in the years he had spent in Germany prior to WWI, and he had taught most of our fighter pilots, including me. Over the years, he had become one of my closest friends.

Over the centuries, Elise had never lost her touch as my tactical offi¬cer. In fact, she had grown even better. Now she wore the same thought¬ful expression she donned whenever she worked on a battle strategy or played chess with me.

"Report," I said to the console hand.

"Sir, ten minutes ago, we detected a Wraith command ship decloak in a very high orbit of the planet, well beyond the reach of the human sat¬ellite. We also detected a Paradine sparrowhawk come out of slip-stream space and Wraith Banshee fighters being launched from the sur-face. Sir, I think it's Shurgal's ship."

Casey and Jen looked at me.

I leaned against the panel, studying the image of the Shurgal's ship. *Shurgal, my old friend, it's nice to see you on this side of the galaxy,* I thought seeing it bore the same battle markings from the invasion of Centaries IV. *It seems that, while we were sent to the past, you were sent to the future.*

I looked at Klaus. "Did they discover our ship's dry dock and the building yard in the Mars orbit?"

He shook his head. "No, we don't think so, but to be on the safe side, they're on high alert and cloaked twenty-four-seven." I nodded.

The alarms went off, then, and I turned back to the holographic screen to see a new ship had joined the space battle. The main super-structure appeared flat, like a big pair of wings broken into sections. The main engine emerged from the middle of the rear. From this angle,

I could just make out two middle sections that jutted in the front. The bridge in the middle was a small bulge.

"Computer, identify," I commanded.

"Wraith specter gunship," said the computer.

We watched eight new blips converge with Shurgal's ship before rapidly shooting off in various directions. I wondered what they could be. As I continued to watch, the specter ship approached one and then moved away twice as fast before righting its course toward the planet.

"Computer, magnify," I commanded, and Shurgal's ship and the specter ship zoomed in. When I saw what had broken off, I blinked. "The Cybersuits," I muttered, as I eyed the pod holograms and embedded thrusters racing for Earth. "Track them! I'm going out to meet them with the retrieval team. I want them given only *human* weapons and clothes! Let me know of their progress!"

From the command center, Jules and I ran all the way to one of the exit hangars, which held land vehicles. In front of a black van was a line of men and women standing at attention.

"Load up!" I ordered while grabbing a long coat from a nearby rack. At once, the van's side door opened, and they all climbed in. I circled to take the front, and Jules followed.

He handed me a holo projector and said, "One last thing." I looked at him. "Come back alive, or your brother will kill me."

Chuckling, I shook my head and climbed into the front passenger seat. "I'll do my best," I said before closing the door with a snap.

At once, the driver started the engine and raced up the ramp.

We sped through the tunnel, and as we approached a solid metrabolium wall built from an alloy ten times stronger than titanium, it opened, and the van jumped through open air and landed on the road. I looked at the side mirrors and saw the camouflaging billboard and trees drop back into place, and then we raced through the city, guided by Jen's directions.

As we neared our destination, I turned to face the group in the back. "Ladies and gents, this is the moment we've waited five-thousand years for." Some faces hardened with determination; a few looked at the people around them. "I want this run by the numbers—in and out! I know we have scores to settle," I continued, "but now is not the time. Right now, our job is to secure the Cybersuits and Shurgal. Everything else is secondary. Is that understood?"

"Yes, sir!" they chorused.

I nodded curtly, but then added solemnly, "Remember, none of us can be captured or left behind."

"Sir!" the driver said suddenly. When I turned to him, he pointed toward eight streaks of light which shot across the sky and came down with a small flash of light in the distance.

"Step on it!" I exclaimed.

"Consider it stepped on, through, around, and under, sir!" The van's engine roared.

Alec

After we followed Officer Anderson to the library, he asked us to sit at a round table by the window. Sighing, I leaned back in my chair to watch the buses leave.

"Looks like we're all walking home," I muttered, setting the chair legs back down.

"Any idea what Plumber is going to have us do?" Blair asked, looking at each of us in turn.

"Maybe he'll take away your weapon of choice," Hunter murmured, and she shot him a dirty look as I stifled a chuckle.

"I don't think many people would find a girl dragging herself through the school halls appealing," Aisha remarked. Turning in Blair's direction, she asked, "Are your foster parents going to give you grief over this?"

"They'll be more worried one of their cash cows might have run off," she murmured in disgust. "They get practically double from the state because of my disability."

"You know you can come to my house and spend the night," Aisha offered. "My parents said you're welcome any time."

Sending her a smile Aisha couldn't see, Blair nodded. "I know," she leaned forward to squeeze her friend's hand, "and if that judge hadn't been a hardass—"

"Language, Miss Blair."

We all groaned and turned to see Plumber stalking over to us. Over his shoulder, we spied Principal Kelly standing in the doorway.

Plumber set his hands down on the table and leaned forward. "For what happened, the lot of you are going to be spending the next six weeks—"

"Six weeks!" we all objected at once.

"But, sir, it was an accident!"

"That's not fair!"

"We didn't have anything to do with it!"

"Come on, Principal Kelly!" I called out, facing the man.

Sighing, he raised his hands and stepped closer.

"One more word and it will be twelve!" Plumber barked, and we all fell silent. "Starting at three sharp, you will all sit in this room for two hours—no excuses, no exceptions! Got it?" I was still smoldering at his words, but we all nodded. "Just count yourselves lucky I was able to talk Bradley's parents out of a lawsuit!" he yelled as he circled the table. "For the next few months, you will all be spending a lot of time together, so I suggest you get used to it! And Blair," she slowly looked up at him, "perhaps one of them will help you curb that temper of yours!" Muttering angrily, he then walked away.

Principal Kelly watched him go with another sigh and then looked back at us. "Give it a little time. I'll probably be able to drop it down to a week," he said, coming closer and placing a hand on Blair's shoulder. "Maybe if you were to vent that frustration in a more positive way, he might be willing...." Letting his words hang, he turned and left.

"So, what are we supposed to do for the next couple of hours?" Hunter moaned, running his hand through his hair.

"You can follow these rules, for starters." We all turned as the librarian appeared. "No talking, no texting, no food, and no phones." She held out a box for our phones.

"You had to ask…" I said, unclipping my phone from its holster and dropping it in.

By the time we were finally released from the library, the sun was going down. We walked down the stairs and Blair wheeled down the ramp.

"So, does anyone here want to call the parents and explain why we're not home yet?" I asked.

As if to answer, every phone but Blair's sounded off. Reflexively, Hunter and I pulled ours out to check the screens.

"Looks like the school took care of it for us," Hunter said, grimacing. "I vote we wait to talk to them until we each get home."

"I guess I'm the only one who doesn't have to worry about parental retribution," Blair said, turning her chair to face us.

Trying not to think about what my parents would do to me when I got home, I silenced my phone. "Well, I vote we take the long way home, past the salvage yard, so we can get our stories straight."

Ian

The van came to a screeching stop outside a walled-up salvage yard. After yanking open the door, I looked up at the sky and saw the faint glow of shifting lights from inside.

"Okay, people, we have a job to do! Let's bring it!" I crouched down and then leaped into the air, flipping over the wall and coming down lightly in a roll. The Centauriens I had selected for this mission landed in crouched positions behind me. "You know what to do!" I barked, and we all tore into the salvage yard.

Alec

"Does anyone have any ideas?" I asked as we walked past lines of wrecked or flattened cars.

"We can always be honest and say it's Blair's fault," Hunter offered.

She reached out and slapped his arm as Aisha said, "Blaming anyone won't help." She waved her unfolded cane left and right so she wouldn't trip on the stray debris, and wished I had chosen the shorter way home.

"Either way," she continued, "if Plumber spoke with our parents, they already know what happened."

"Then does it even matter what we say?" I asked, feeling them all looking at me. We stepped past an open area with cars and scrap metal piled high in all directions.

"The day we stay silent is the day people will walk all over us," Blair said maneuvering her chair.

Sighing, Hunter stepped in front of her. "Look, Miss X-23, I get the thing about not letting people walk all over you, but—"

"What's that sound?" Aisha interrupted.

"What sound?" I asked, grateful for the change of subject, so I wouldn't have to scrape Hunter off the ground after Blair had run him over.

"Listen," Aisha said, tilting her head to the side.

We all fell silent, and I closed my eyes and focused on the sounds of the night around me. Then I heard it: a faint roar that sounded far off but was quickly becoming louder. My eyes snapped open, and I looked left and right. The volume increased, but I couldn't find the source of the roar until I looked up into the night sky.

"Run!" I yelled when I saw the fiery streaks of light coming down at us.

Without even thinking, I scooped Aisha into my arms and high-tailed it toward a large, white van on cinderblocks at the edge of the yard. Behind me, Hunter ran, pushing Blair's chair, to catch up. Behind the van, I threw myself across Aisha just as the ground was rocked by impact and the heatwave of an explosion. Dirt showered down on and around us, along with other debris.

When everything had finally settled, I lifted my head; dirt slid down my neck and back. As I looked around, I saw a few rows of cars and heaps of scrap metal had been knocked down, as well as that we had almost been crushed by a wrecked SUV now leaning precariously against the van.

At once, Aisha tore herself out of my arms and darted away from the van. Hunter and Blair weren't far behind, the latter helping the former with rapid pushes on the wheel handles.

"Alec, what's going on? What happened?" Aisha asked. Before I could reply, the weight of the SUV tipped the van over, and both vehicles crashed to the ground. "What was that?" Aisha asked, her voice rising with alarm.

"A couple cars fell over, that's all," I said reassuringly.

"Was it a meteorite?" she asked, extending her cane with a flick of her wrist.

"I'm not sure." I then turned and stared, open-mouthed, at what looked like five oval pods with sharp points directed at the sky. The pods were made of a metal that seemed to shift under the starlight, and colored lights flashed at the top and middle as steam issued from vents.

"Those aren't meteorites," Hunter said in shocked awe. Blair just stared in wonder.

"What do you mean they aren't meteorites?" Aisha moved forward, her cane sweeping left and right. She stopped when the tip of her cane tapped one of the pods. "Wha—?" She tapped a couple more times, each one higher than the one before. "Allah, what is this?" Aisha slowly raised one hand and placed it against the metal surface.

I charged forward, seized her by the wrist, and jerked her hand away. "Careful! It will…" I paused when I flipped her hand over, "burn you." Her hand was undamaged and cool to the touch; slowly, I looked up to her face, which was turned in my direction.

Before any of us could speak again, I heard a hissing sound and turned to see a section of the pod begin to open. Still holding Aisha by the wrist, I pulled her back as all the pods suddenly opened like flowers. Standing in the middle of each pod was what looked like an armored human figure, a blank piece of metal where the face should have been.

"What the heck are those?" Hunter asked, moving closer.

"No idea," I answered, just as stunned.

"Would one of you tell me what has you so shocked?" Aisha asked.

As I described every detail, we all moved closer to get a better look. Suddenly, from where the eyes should have been on the figures, a wide beam shot out in our direction. We jumped back, and the beam moved from the top of our heads down to our feet and back up again.

When the light went out, Hunter, Blair, and I shared a look. We then jolted back as the figures opened up, revealing empty shells. One lowered itself to lie flat on the ground before opening like the others.

"What's going on?" Aisha asked. "What were those sounds?"

"I think," I said, my mind running wild with the possibilities, "I think these things just scanned us… and now they want us to hop in."

"What do we do?" Hunter asked, looking at me.

For a second, I just looked at him, but then I caught movement directly behind him. "Blair!" I called as she wheeled herself to the shell on the ground. "What are you doing?" I demanded as she locked her wheels in place.

"No guts, no glory," she said, pushing herself out of her chair and landing flat on her chest next to the figure. She crawled forward, and before we could stop her, she rolled over and into the shell.

Hunter and I watched in horror as whatever that thing was closed, sealing her inside. "Blair!" I yelled, dropping down and pounding my fist on the figure's chest. "Blair, answer me!" I raised my fist again.

In a flash, the figure sat up, seizing my fist. "You can stop yelling," an altered voice said through the face piece.

Blinking, I stared in stunned silence. "Are you all right?"

Blair silently examined her armor-covered hands. "So far, everything seems all right," she said.

She turned her attention to her legs, and following her gaze, I watched as the appendages gave the smallest twitch. I barely heard her emit a small sound of surprise as she gradually climbed to her feet, her movements slow and tentative. Her blank metal face looked around at us as she laughed in small, grateful bursts.

"Blair? Blair, what's happening?" Aisha asked, moving forward.

"I'm standing," the girl said simply in a light, happy voice before cautiously taking a step. "I'm walking," she continued.

Aisha grinned wide and then stepped forward. When she was close to one of the figures, she folded her cane and, reaching with her hands, turned and backed into the figure.

As with Blair, the shell closed around her, and for a couple of seconds, it was still. Aisha then gave a cry of surprise and froze with her armored hands in front of her.

"Aisha?" I asked, stepping forward. "Are you okay?"

She simply stood there, flexing and opening her hands several times, and then she slowly faced me. Eventually, she took a few small steps closer. "Alec," she asked, also in an altered voice, "is that you?"

Eyebrow lifting, I nodded. "Yeah," I said slowly. "Is something wrong?"

Slowly, she shook her head. "No, I think something's *right* because, praise be to Allah, for the first time in my life, I think I can see," she said.

Ian

Turkey peeking around each corner, I moved silently through the rows of stacked cars and scrap metal. I pressed myself flat against the side of a vehicle and turned my watch on. As I pressed the sides, a holographic image appeared above it, and I quickly scanned the latest information the base had sent to me.

"Reminds me of the labyrinth," I muttered. "A few more corners and I'm there." Checking carefully, I slipped around the next corner and the last and then froze.

Before me was Shurgal's ship. The outer skin carried signs that it had gone through battle, including scars from blaster fire. A section had been blown away, revealing the cargo hold. There, sprawled on the ground with his wings in awkward positions, was Shurgal.

"Shurgal!" I exclaimed as I raced toward him. Skidding on my knees, I turned him over, relieved to see he was still breathing. "Shurgal! Shurgal, wake up!" I snapped at him, tapping his face.

With a groan, he slowly opened his eyes. "Ian," he said weakly, "you're alive. How is that possible?"

"I'll explain later," I said, turning the dial on my watch and pressing the sides again. "El Dorado, this is Ian," I said as the holographic face of one of the techs appeared. "I have Shurgal—"

He seized my wrist, and I was surprised by the force of his grip given his weakened condition. "Ian," he whispered and slowly pointed to the blown-open ship. "Seven fell... Arina... one... go." His arm then fell limp at his side.

Biting my lip, I looked down at him. He wasn't dead, but he certainly needed medical help as soon as possible. I raised my gaze to the hole and then looked back at my friend. "I'll be right back, I promise," I said before climbing to my feet.

I darted to the hole and looked into the ship, where the floor was covered in debris and equipment. There, against the far wall, was one of the Cybersuit pods.

I pulled myself through the hole and maneuvered toward it before I pressed my hand against the cool, metal surface. I then stepped back, and the sections opened with a hiss, revealing the suit inside.

I blinked in surprise as a beam of light scanned me and then, as I remembered from so long ago, the suit opened. Drawing back my shoulders, I took a deep breath, walked forward, and stepped inside. As I took my place, the suit sealed itself closed, and I was surrounded in darkness.

"Pilot entry complete. DNA coding locked," a computerized voice said in my ear. "Neuronic pilot interface commencing," the voice said in my ear, and I felt something soft and squishy press against the back of my neck. The area before my eyes suddenly lit up, and I could once more see the ship's hold as sensor readouts appeared in the corners and ran along the sides of my vision. "Activating motor drives. Power up complete."

Slowly, I looked down at my armored hands, which curled into fists, and stepped out of the pod and through the hole, which I pounded larger to accommodate the armor.

Outside, I quickly returned to Shurgal's side. "Come on, we've got to get out of here!" I said as I picked him up. "We can't wait for help to arrive!"

With a moan, he slowly opened one eye. "It looks good on you," he said.

Chuckling, I shook my head. "How can you tell when you can't see my face? Now let's get you some medical attention."

"Ian," he said weakly, "you must… find them."

I blinked. "Don't worry, buddy. I have a team here with me—we'll find the other Cybersuits," I said reassuringly.

"No," he said, even weaker, "you must find… family."

His words stopped me in my tracks. "Family?" I repeated. "Arina?" I asked, I asked thinking of his daughter and only living family member after the death of his wife. "Arina was with you?" Shurgal, however, had already gone limp again.

"Shurgal, Shurgal!" I said, shaking him lightly, trying to wake him.

When he didn't open his eyes, I let loose a light curse. I've got to get him back to Eldorado for medical attention, but with my wrist . . .

I froze when I saw series of numbers run from bottom to top on the screen. Then the words Link Established flashed across the screen.

Before I had time to ponder what was going on, a holographic version of Casey's face appeared on the screen.

I froze when I saw series of numbers run from the bottom to the top of the screen, and then the words Link Established flashed across it.

Before I had time to ponder what was going on, a holographic version of Casey's face appeared on the screen.

"Ian, what the heck just happened? Our system was just hacked!"

"I think it was the suit," I said.

"You're in a suit?" Casey asked, and a giant grin spread across his face as I heard cheers in the background.

"Yeah. Now, get Doc warmed up—I may be coming in hot with a medical emergency. I rendezvoused with the rest of the team, so we can return to El Dorado," I said.

I followed a map readout of the yard toward a series of nearby moving blips. When I got close, I frowned. Although I couldn't yet see anyone, I heard a lot of cheering and the crashing and bending of metal.

"They're making enough noise to wake the dead," I growled. With

Shurgal still in my arms, I rounded the last corner and what I saw stopped me in my tracks.

A Cybersuited figure flipped through the air as another yelled, "Check this out!" Turning, it drove its fist into the side of a car, pulling out the rear axle.

"Iron Man, eat your heart out!" it said as it bent the axle like a pretzel before tossing it aside. "Oh, yeah!"

At the top of another pile of cars, another armored figure lifted a whole SUV above its head. "Just call me Supergirl!" it declared before tossing the wreck aside with a crash.

A fourth figure stood, rooted, staring up at the stars.

Pushing aside my surprise, I yelled, "Aten-hut!"

At once, they all turned to look at me. "Front and center, people! This was supposed to be done by the numbers!" I stepped into clear view. "Simple retrieval, which means no showing off or test drives!"

Slowly, two of them looked at each other.

"Uh, who are you?" one asked, pointing at me.

Blinking, I marched right up to the figure. "Name and rank!"

For a second, silence reigned before the figure shrank back. "Uh, do these belong to you?" it asked, pointing at me again.

My eyes widened.

"Our bad," said the first.

"What the heck is that?" the one with the female voice asked, dropping down and pointing at Shurgal.

In stunned silence, I looked from one armored figure to another.

"Commander," one of my team members said over the comm, "we found the pods! They're empty—no sign of the suits! All one group found is a wheelchair."

"I know," I muttered back. "Grab the chair and get back to base."

"What about the Cybersuits, sir?"

"Don't worry," I answered, looking from one figure to another. "They're right in front of me," I could almost hear my team freeze, "and they already have people inside them."

CHAPTER 6

FRIEND OR FOE

Alec

Before my mind could fully process Aisha's revelation, a sharp *beeee! beeee! beeee!* sounded in my ear.

"What's happening?" I said, but no one answered. Parts of the view screen flashed red, and in the bottom corner, red dots appeared on the map, moving right at us.

At once, Mr. Military Talk spun in the direction of whatever was heading our way. "Incoming!" he barked. He then turned and dropped the birdman into my arms. "Protect him!" he snapped quietly. "Now go!" A shadow moved behind him, quickly followed by flashlight beams. "Go!" he snapped again, shoving me. "I'll catch up!" He then jerked into position and stood with his arms straight at his side.

"Let's go!" I hissed, and we all darted down the opposite path.

Ian

My eyes were the only parts of my body that moved as I focused on the corner the beams of light came from. The sound of voices carried through the night air. An audio symbol appeared on the screen, and above it flashed **Audio Amplified**. Voices arrived through my earpieces.

A male voice said, "I heard Kizor was spitting nails, as the humans say, when that ship slipped through."

"Then he's in for a rude awakening." This time, the voice was female. "I heard Kizor threw the gunner who let the ship through out of the airlock."

Now I don't have to hunt you across the stars, Kizor, I thought as my face hardened with hate.

A man and woman dressed in normal civilian clothes appeared from around the corner, holding flashlights in one hand and Wraith pulse blasters in the other. Before I could decide what to do, a Zorvain appeared in front of me like shimmering water with a sound that reminded me of shuffling cards. I couldn't help but grin at this stroke of good luck.

"You were supposed to stay camouflaged!" the woman said to the Zorvain, and then both possessed humans froze.

For a couple of seconds, they just stared at me, and then a toothy, predatory smile spread across the man's face. "Looks like this night won't be wasted, after all," he said, walking up to me. "Once we present this to Overlord Kizor, we could very well be promoted to Lords, ourselves."

"Basarla," the possessed Zorvain growled, "you forget we were the ones who captured it!"

"Wrong!" I said, seizing him by the throat.

Slowly, I lifted the struggling Zorvain off its feet, and *DNA Acquisition Complete* flashed across the screen. As a rotating image of a Zorvain, along with several variations, appeared in front of me, I jerked him toward me and yelled, "I've got you!" My right mechanical hand shrunk into my forearm before it shifted into an emitter. The energy sword that shot out cut through the Zorvain like a hot knife through butter. "I'm sorry," I whispered. "May your ancestors welcome you with honor at the Home Tree of the Gods." I then let him drop to the ground on his side, dead.

Before the man and woman could react, I quickly raised my left arm, which reshaped into a buster cannon. *I hope I can keep them alive,* I thought as my face screen read *Sonic Stun Activated.*

To my surprise, the charge section of the cannon slid out and spread like a dish. When I fired on the humans, a small, circular wave of almost transparent air shot at them with a low hum, lifting the pair off their feet and slamming them against the rack of cars behind them.

As they fell to the ground, I just stared. "That's a new feature," I muttered. "I don't envy the headaches they'll have when they wake up."

One at a time, I picked them up, wrapped metal bars around their arms and legs, and tossed them into the trunk of a wrecked car. I then shut the trunk to lock them in.

Alec

We ran between the rows of cars, the birdman still in my arms. "Does anyone have any idea what just happened?" I asked.

"I'm still trying to process the fact that you're carrying a creature that looks like an angel!" Hunter answered.

"You know what we're fixated on!" Blair said next to me. At her side, Aisha turned her head every which way as she tried to see everything around her.

The question is how the heck is Blair able to walk and Aisha able to see? I thought.

"Look!" Aisha suddenly shouted, pointing.

I skidded to a stop and looked up just in time to see a figure silhouetted against the moon overhead. With a snap, a pair of wings opened, and it dropped down toward us.

It landed on one knee, wings partially open, and then stood slowly, its faceless head surveying us. I shifted the birdman into Aisha's arms and moved to the front of the group.

The winged figure's head tilted, as if it were puzzled.

Before either of us could make a move, a line of spikes embedded themselves in the ground at its feet. Jerking back, it looked up, and before I could follow suit, the figure who had first handed me the birdman dropped down in front of us. It, however, looked different now, with the textured surface of the metal looking almost reptilian with smooth, oval ridges on his forearms, legs, shoulders, back, and head.

"Don't give me another reason to kill you, Kizor!" our strange acquaintance growled. His voice was altered, but his tone was serious as sharp spikes grew from its now excessively large forearm.

The winged figure held our acquaintance's gaze and straightened. "You think I'm Kizor?" it demanded.

After a moment, our acquaintance seemed to relax. "Arina? Arina, is that you?" it asked.

Before the winged figure could answer, a third armored figure dropped out of the sky, landing on one knee on top of a pile of cars. It stood erect, surveying us all. As its eyes flashed red, a chill ran down my spine. Even though I'd just laid eyes on this… whatever, it somehow felt twisted, dark, and dangerous—evil, even.

"Well, well," it said in a digital voice, "I was hoping to retrieve both the ship and its cargo, but now that I know what and who was in that ship, I'm doubly disappointed."

Slowly, our acquaintance moved closer to the other winged figure.

Ian

I moved toward the winged Paradine in the Cybersuit and muttered so Kizor wouldn't hear, "Get them out of here," I nodded toward the still unidentified group. "They're not soldiers."

The winged figure held my gaze for a moment before glancing the four. "I'll take care of them," it said, and I sighed in relief, "but I'm not taking the one they're holding."

"You would leave one of your own behind?"

Before it could reply, Kizor growled, "It's of no consequence if I can't capture any of you—I will ensure that those Cybersuits won't be used against me!" Around him, more Zorvains appeared as they decamouflaged from their hiding spots.

I quietly said to the Paradine, "Fine, I'll take him, but you just made my job a lot harder!" Quickly, I snatched Shurgal into my arms and darted away.

"Stop him!" Kizor shouted behind me. "He has the creator of the Cybersuit!"

"No chance in hell, Kizor!" I yelled back, running even faster as clawed footsteps pounded behind me.

CHAPTER 7

LEAP OF FAITH

Alec

The figure our acquaintance had just called Kizor yelled, "If they escape, this place will be dripping with your blood!"

By this point, a bunch of lizard-like creatures had appeared out of nowhere. Now a few followed Kizor, but about ten stayed behind and slowly advanced.

"So, um… what do we do?" I asked the winged figure who still stood in front of us.

"Do any of you know how to fight?" it asked, glancing over its shoulder at us. We answered with silence. "Then we do the only thing we can do," it said, turning toward the lizard creatures. "Run!" With two great flaps of its wings, it rose in the air.

I glanced back at the lizard creatures as they drew their weapons and needed no further encouragement. "Move it!" I yelled, and we all turned and ran.

Behind us, I heard the clawed feet of the lizard creatures pursuing us. With my arms pumping wildly, I stopped myself from looking back to see if they were still on our tails. As we rounded a bend, a fork in the path between the wrecked and flattened cars loomed ahead.

"Split up!" I called to the others. "They can't chase all of us at the same time!" At once, Aisha and Blair tore down one pathway; Hunter and I dashed down the other.

Around the next corner, I skidded to a stop and peered back. Our pursuers paused, looking down one path and then the other, and then they split up.

After I caught up with Hunter, he asked, "How close?"

"Do you really want to know?"

Around another corner, a wall loomed before us. My attention was caught by a whooshing sound, and I looked up and saw the winged figure swoop low. "Any chance for some air support?" I shouted up.

He rolled to one side and dove. Sweeping with his wing, he knocked down a pile of cars and soared into the air. I heard the lizard creatures scream as they were crushed by the falling heaps, buried under twisted, crushed metal.

"You think it got them all?" Hunter asked, jabbing his thumb toward the figure still in the air.

"Go help the others!" I called to it. It nodded and its wings arched, lifting the figure in the direction the girls had gone. Suddenly, pulsing beams of light rose toward the retreating figure. "Does that answer your question?" I asked hunter.

I looked at the wall behind us, and as more of the lizard creatures climbed over the crushed pile, said, "I vote we see just how high we can jump in these things!"

"You've got my vote!" Hunter said.

We squatted low and then leaped into the air. Higher and higher we went, and I held my breath, eyes on the edge of the wall above us, hopeful we would make it. We passed the top of the wall and kept ascending, and then my arms and legs began to flail. My heart seemed to skip a beat as I looked down at the still-shrinking ground.

"Do you think we're going to have to worry about getting hit by an airplane?" Hunter shouted next to me.

As if to answer his question, a spaceship materialized out of nowhere, turning its side to face us and slowly opening a hatch. Astounded, I saw a man and a lizard creature in the doorway, evil grins of triumph on their faces.

"I think we just leaped to our own capture!" I said to Hunter.

Suddenly, large, metallic spears with feather-like tips shot through the air and embedded into the side of ship around the hatch. At once, the man and lizard creature jerked backward, disappearing inside. I glanced in the direction the spears had come from to find the winged figure approaching. Abruptly, it dropped back to the ground, and the feather-like tips of the metallic spears exploded above us.

Hunter and I both screamed as we suddenly dropped, our arms and legs acting like windmill sails as we flipped through the air. The ground raced up to meet us, and we crashed through the top and bottom of a van and came to a halt in a small crater in the ground.

Before I could catch my breath, someone yanked the van doors open with such force that the doors ripped free.

"Are you two all right?" one of the girls yelled at the gaping hole in the middle of the floor.

Hunter moaned beside me, "I'm glad we're wearing armor, because that belly flop would have really hurt."

"Is everyone all right?" the winged figure called out above us. I nodded, and it said, "Good. Let's get the heck out of here!"

"Come on!" I shouted. "If we follow, we might get out of here!" My friends lined up behind me with the figure in the air leading the way.

Ian

My first thought was to get Shurgal out of sight. I slid the door of a wrecked van open and placed him gently inside. "Stay safe, my friend," I said as his head rolled to its side, "and stay quiet." I slid the door closed on the unconscious Paradine and darted away.

The Zorvains appeared around the bend and started chasing me. At the end of the lane, I jumped up onto the nearest pile of cars and landed in a roll before grabbing a Zorvain by the back of the neck and throwing him on the pile. He crashed against several wrecks before he dropped to the ground next to the crusher. Spinning, I kicked another in the face, propelling him and the one behind him backward.

When I heard a sound behind me, I whipped around in time to duck beneath the slash of the bladed spike that extended from a Zorvain's arm. Feeling identical spikes emerge along my arm, I slashed him across the side before stabbing him in the back with the spikes. With my arm raised, I blocked the blow from the figure behind him.

"You will be ours, or you will not survive the night!" it threatened in its native tongue. Then it looked down at the buster cannon I had pressed to its midsection.

"You first!" I hissed and then fired. As the Zorvain dropped, I turned. When I saw Kizor right before me, I froze.

"You're good," he said as we circled each other. "I don't know which I would enjoy more," his forearm reshaped itself and his energy sword shot out, "killing you or capturing you and having you possessed."

I recalled the invasion of Centauries, and my fingers twitched, itching for the fight to come. I then thought of Shurgal and my face went slack. *If I don't get him back to base for immediate medical attention, he might die.*

In a flash, I raised my cannon-bearing arm and fired. Reacting just as fast, Kizor lifted his opposite arm and blocked the shot with a shield. He then twisted away, narrowly dodging the whip that had been at my hip as it shot past him.

"You missed!" he said with a cackle, but then his head whipped around and he stared at the far end of the whip coiled around the lever of a crane. His eyes traveled up the arm of the crane.

"Remember the old saying about flying through space?" I snapped, pulling back on the whip before throwing myself against the car under me, my spikes lodging into the metal.

Behind me, I heard Kizor cry out in shock and outrage.

Clang!

Looking back, I nearly lost control at the sight of Kizor, his arms spread wide, stuck to the bottom of the now-humming electromagnet high above me.

"The bigger or closer you are to a sun, the faster you burn," I muttered before I retracted the spikes and dragged myself to the edge of the car's roof. Once on the ground, I jogged back the way I came.

I returned to Shurgal and climbed in the van, wrapping him in my arms. *Chameleon, chameleon*, I thought hoping it would work. With a snapping sound, like playing cards on bike spokes, the skin on the Cybersuit changed to blend into the area around me.

A second later, I heard Kizor scream at someone to set him free. The humming from the magnet stopped; a moment later, he charged into my line of sight with several possessed Zorvains in tow.

"He's gone, my lord."

Kizor released a cry of rage, and his forearm formed into an energy sword. Spinning, he slashed out at the one who'd spoken, and that Zorvain's head went flying.

"Does anyone else want to point out their obvious failures?" he growled with all the coziness of a hissing cobra.

Shifting a little, I saw another group of Zorvains come down the pathway from the opposite direction. "My lord! The others got away!" one of them reported.

With the same cry, Kizor spun and sent that speaker's head flying, as well. As he looked from one group to the other and they shrank away, I could sense his satisfaction.

"We're done here!" he growled. "We must leave before we're discovered. Send in possessed humans to clean up!" With a low growl, his Paradine wings lifted him into the sky as the Zorvains dispersed.

After a moment of silence and the readouts confirmed the coast was clear, I slowly emerged from the van with Shurgal.

"Now I need your help, old friend," I said, even though I knew he couldn't hear me, as I absorbed his DNA and grew Paradine wings. Seconds later, I carried him through the sky, soaring above the clouds.

CHAPTER 8

A SON'S RAGE

Alec

We followed the winged figure to the edge of the scrap yard, where it came to a stop.

"What are we supposed to do now? Call a taxi?" I demanded.

As if in response, a van skidded to a stop right in front of us and the side door slid open. "Get in if you want to live!" a voice shouted from inside.

I hesitated for the briefest of seconds, with all of my parents' old warnings about stranger danger racing through my head. What, however, could be stranger than the situation we were already in? I quickly nodded at my friends, and we all piled in. As soon as Aisha jumped inside, the door slammed home, the engine roared, and the van shot forward.

Ian

I gagged the Wraith-possessed humans still bound by the metal I had bent around them, placed Shurgal over my shoulder, and carried all three to the edge of the forest on the outskirts of the city. When I placed them on the forest floor, the possessed humans issued what I could only guess were muffled insults—the gags made their oaths incoherent.

"I may not know exactly what you're saying," I said, moving forward, "but I have a feeling it's not that nice."

I pressed on the knot of an old oak, and the pair fell silent as a circle of earth rose up near the great tree, revealing a metal tube which shone in the moonlight.

With a hiss, two sections slid open, revealing a hollow interior large enough to hold them both. "Then again," I remarked, stepping forward, "you're possessed, and from what I know of Wraiths, they're not very diplomatic." I picked them up off the ground and dragged them into the elevator, where I let them slump to their knees as we descended rapidly underground. When the doors opened again, we were met by a med team holding blaster rifles, as well as a security detachment.

"Commander!" the head of the med team said, a stretcher hovering behind him between the other two medics.

"Get Shurgal to medical now!" I barked, gently lying the unconscious Paradine down on the stretcher.

"And these two?" Lieutenant Anella, in charge of the security detail, asked, jabbing the man with her rifle.

Turning, I looked at the bound man and woman. "Possessed by Wraiths." At once, the entire security force turned, their weapons trained on the pair, with looks of disgust, hatred, and pity on all of their faces. "Lower your weapons!" I ordered. The team in front of me looked at each other before glancing at me. "Lower your weapons!" I said more firmly.

For a second, none of them moved, but then they slowly relaxed and lowered their weapons a fraction. I could tell they still had itchy trigger fingers.

"Lieutenant Anella," standing straight, she faced me, weapon presented, "escort these two to the brig!" I growled. "They are to be unharmed... and unspoiled," I instructed.

"Yes, sir, Commander!" she said with a brisk nod.

Slowly, I turned to face the pair again. "One wrong move, though," I added before looking back at Lieutenant Anella, "and shoot 'em."

"Sir!" she nodded. Her soldiers surrounded the pair and released their metal bindings before escorting them out.

I watched them disappear from my line of sight through a set of sliding doors, and then I turned to walk through another set of doors. It was time to see Karl.

As I walked down the hall, people stopped what they were doing, most looking awestruck or hopeful as I passed in the Cybersuit.

When I arrived at the engineering department, activity ceased in the main research and development room as all eyes turned to me. I scanned their faces briefly before I walked toward a wide-eyed Karl.

"I have something for you to work on," I said. With the sound of sliding metal, my suit opened. "Merry Christmas." I stepped out. "Get to work on it and begin mass production, and I expect your best."

"Yes, sir!" Karl snapped to attention with a salute, and the people around us cheered.

When I was finally able to leave, I quickly met up with Jules, Casey, Klaus, Damon, and Jen, who bombarded me with questions about what happened. When I told them about Shurgal, they were shocked. I asked them to pull up any available information on what had been recovered from the crash site, and then I went to my quarters.

I restarted the movie, pulled out another bottle of scotch and a glass, and turned to the holographic version of Terra. "So, honey, where were we?"

Alec

Crouched in the back of the van, I tried to get a good look at the driver as we roared down the street. She had a single long braid down her back, but she kept her eyes on the road.

Behind me, someone whispered, "Do you get the feeling that we might have made a mistake?" We all looked and sounded so alike in our suits, I wasn't sure who was who.

"You shouldn't worry too much," the driver said without turning. "You all pack enough firepower to take out an army." As I stared at my friends, the driver continued, "Okay, maybe a human army. I must say, I may have met a Paradine, but this is a first for your kind."

"What did we get ourselves into?" I asked aloud. Even my own voice sounded strange through the mask.

My friends just shrugged.

"That's what I would like to know, as well!" the driver said as the van took a sharp turn around a corner. "Who are you? Are you Centauriens? Did you come here with Shurgal? Is he alive? Is he safe?"

"What are Centauriens?" I guessed the voice belonged to Aisha.

"Who the heck is Shurgal?" I guessed that one belonged to Blair.

The driver slammed on the brakes, and we all lost our balance, knocking into each other with loud clangs. The driver whipped her head toward us.

"You're human!" she said, her eyes wide.

"Last I checked," Hunter said, righting himself. "Have you looked in the mirror lately? So are you!"

She either ignored or didn't hear the sarcastic comment as she continued to stare at us. "How did this happen?" she finally muttered. "Where is Shurgal?"

"It would help if we knew who Shurgal was!" I said.

With a jerk, she turned to face the windshield again. "Not here—it's not safe." She put the van back in motion. "At least I know you're not possessed by Wraiths."

"What are Wraiths?" I demanded.

She didn't answer. In fact, for the rest of the ride, she was silent, despite our repeated attempts to try to get her to talk to us. She kept her eyes locked on the road.

When we turned out of the city, I started to worry.

"Any idea where she's taking us?" Hunter asked as I gazed out the window. "We should have thought of that before we got in the van."

"What? You think we can't take her if we have to?" I asked, jabbing my thumb at the driver.

"Guys," we all looked at Blair, "is it just me or are we going faster?"

I glanced out the window and at once I realized she was right. Not only that, but the lady was now driving on loose rock, toward what seemed to be some kind of quarry.

"Look!" Hunter said, whipping around. I followed his pointing finger to see the woman was driving toward a solid rock wall at top speed.

"Lady, are you crazy?" I cried, reaching for the wheel.

Before I could grab it to turn us away from the impending crash, however, the wall was gone. I released short, rapid breaths and turned around to see it slide closed the second the van cleared.

"Well, that just knocked ten years off my life," Hunter said, slumping against the van wall.

"Compared to what you all stumbled into," the woman said as she slowed to drive safely through a twisting tunnel, "you have a lot more to worry about than a camouflaged entrance."

That's not ominous, I thought. "Who do you think you are, lady? Batwoman?"

She looked at me in the rearview mirror. "I prefer Pythia for now," she answered.

In what seemed like no time, the van came to a screeching halt. "Get out!" she snapped as she reached over to the passenger seat and pulled a pair of crutches toward her. She opened the driver's side door, and after slipping her upper arms into the grips, she got out.

We all stared at each other in surprise and wonder until Blair said, "It's not the strangest thing to happen to us tonight."

We all filed out and lined up next to each other. For a moment, I simply stared into the darkness, but then a message flashed across my helmet view screen: *Night Vision Activated.*

The area around us became bright, as if it were the middle of the day, and Pythia's voice called out, "Lights!"

At once, my hands reflexively rose to try to block the blinding light of the screen.

"I take it the night vision was activated," Pythia said, stepping into view. "Fawkes," she called out next.

At once, the readouts in front of me turned red, and the suit froze. "Hey!" I yelled. "I can't move!"

"None of us can!" Blair said.

"It's a failsafe built into these models," Pythia explained, looking at us all. "It paralyzes the suits, in case they fall into the wrong hands."

For the first time, I looked around the room. The far rock wall was filled with what looked like an advanced supercomputer with multiple screens of various sizes. Equally advanced equipment was dotted here and there throughout the room.

"Are you some kind of government scientist?" Hunter demanded.

She looked at him. "These were built for the government," she confirmed, "but not the one you're thinking of."

She turned away from us at the sound of flapping, and the winged figure landed in front of her. "I see you found them," it said, looking us over.

"Did you get Shurgal?" she asked. "Where is he?"

Slowly, the figure turned its gaze on her. "No," it said before turning away.

Fast on her crutches, Pythia hobbled in front of the figure to stop it. "What do you mean?" she demanded. "Was he dead? What happened?"

"Are you talking about that bird guy?" Hunter asked.

Pythia turned her attention to him. "You saw him?" she asked, and I could hear the emotion in her voice. "Was he alive?"

"Yeah, he was alive—unconscious, but alive," Hunter continued. "Your friend, here, didn't want to even touch him."

"What?" the woman snapped. She turned to face the winged figure again, as if she were scolding a child. "You just left him? How could you?" she said, rapping the figure on the arm with her crutch. She stumbled, and the creature caught her before she fell.

"How could I?" it asked, straightening. "How could you?" it continued, walking over and gently setting Pythia down in a chair. "Shurgal abandoned us when the MS started affecting your legs." The figure made sure she was comfortable before it straightened. "He *doesn't* love or care about us, Mom."

"Mom?" I asked, staring at the pair. At once, everything seemed to snap into place in my mind. "Gavin?" I asked the winged figure as it slowly turned to look at me. "Is that you, Gavin?"

For a few moments, he just looked at me, but then his suit opened with a hiss. "How do you know me?" Gavin asked, stepping out. When he fully emerged from the suit, my eyes just about popped out of my head. He stood straight and tall, a pair of powerful wings attached to his back.

"How do you know me?" he asked, eyeing us.

When we remained silent, the woman said, "Incubator!"

The next thing we knew, our suits opened with a hiss, and a loud thump reverberated through the air. Stepping out, I looked over and saw Blair sprawled on the ground.

"Blair, are you all right?" Aisha called. Unfolding her cane with a flick of her wrist, she turned toward her friend.

"Kids?" the woman exclaimed, and I turned back to see her stunned face. "Not only humans—kids!"

"The word is *teenagers*!" Blair said, lifting her chest off the ground. "Now, are you going to get me a chair, or am I going to have to drag myself to one?"

"Gavin!" the woman said, looking at her son.

He promptly moved forward and, with what seemed like little effort, picked Blair up in his arms. As he carried her toward a chair next to his mother, Blair blinked up at him. "So… should we ask who your father is?"

"I'd think that would be obvious," Gavin replied with a flex of his wings.

"I take it you have daddy issues," she said as he set her down gently.

He glared at her. "You would, too, if your father abandoned your family for more than ten years," he said, turning his back to her.

"Gavin, he didn't abandon us!" Pythia snapped, pulling herself to her feet. "He had to deliver the Cybersuits!"

"Then where the heck has he been since?" he demanded, whipping around to glare at her.

"Uh, excuse me?" We all stopped to look at Hunter. "Can we get a direct flight back to reality, or would one of you let us know what the heck is going on?" He said with a few waves of his hands. "I mean, first we were nearly crushed by these things falling out of the sky," he paused to jab his thumb at the suits, "and then we get chased by giant lizard creatures…"

"And what looked like living liquid," Blair added.

"Living liquid?" Gavin's mother gasped. "Did it change shape?"

Blair nodded. "I punched it once in the head and it reshaped itself. It caught my wrist in its body by moving its head to the side."

"Sloozes," Pythia said. "It's a shapeshifter race that resembles living liquid. They were one of the early victims of the Wraiths' conquests." She turned to Gavin and said, "This situation just keeps getting worse."

He replied, "Luckily, they can only become something of equal mass, but they can also go from being soft as pillows to hard as diamonds in a split second. Like the Zorvains, they can form their own weapons, too."

I cleared my throat. "Not that this isn't fascinating, but what happens next? Will these creatures return to their planet? Should we all just go home?"

Pythia stared at me. "First things first," she said as she nodded at Gavin. "Give him your parents' numbers so we can let them know where you are and provide you with a cover story. They must be worried sick."

"Not mine." We all looked at Blair. "The last kid who ran away wasn't reported for a week—and only because the social worker visited."

"Runaway? Social worker?" Gavin's mother asked.

"The glorious life of foster care," Blair replied with a shrug.

For a second, Pythia was silent. "We'll need their number, anyway. Now, for the rest of you," she turned to us, "the sooner you give us your numbers, the sooner I can fill you in on what you've accidently stumbled into."

CHAPTER 9

THE COMING STORM

Alec

When Gavin left to call our parents with the story that we were spending the night at his house, we gathered around his mother.

"So, start talking," I said after I led Aisha to a chair.

Pythia moved toward the round table in the middle of the room. "Simply put, you have found yourself in the middle of an intergalactic war," she stated. She pushed some buttons that lit up, and a hologram of the Milky Way Galaxy sprang to life above the table.

For the next ten minutes, Gavin's mother told us a tale that seemed to belong in a sci-fi novel of an alien parasitic race called Wraiths that was sweeping across the stars, enslaving entire planets as they went.

"A couple weeks after the Zorvains arrived back home from that uncharted world, their allies received both a distress call and a quarantine from their jungle-like home world. Ships were sent to investigate, and then contact was lost with the rescue parties.

"When contact finally reestablished, they were elated that our investigation and rescue parties were safe. That, however, was before the surviving refugees told of the coming nightmare and what had been unleashed from that new world.

"The peaceful race that had first been encountered were, in fact, possessed by a ghost-like, parasitic race: the Wraiths. They absorb into the body of their host, completely taking over their mind.

"Shortly after the Wraiths arrived on the Zorvainian home world, they started taking over. Soon, it was impossible to tell who was an untouched Zorvain and who was actually a Wraith in disguise. Once the free populace of the planet learned what was happening, they started fighting back and tried to call for help. Without a way to identify who was an enemy and who was a friend, however, the Zorvains couldn't mount a counteroffensive, and so they fell."

She took a deep breath and then explained how the campaign had been marred by one defeat after another as Wraiths spread throughout the stars, taking planet after planet, most not even realizing they had been invaded until it was too late. Nothing seemed to slow them down, let alone stop them.

Next, she told us about Shurgal, a scientist, explorer, and warrior who'd planned to build something that would help turn the tide. He had searched for a place he could hide his work from the Wraiths and discovered a planet mostly made of water with a people ignorant of what lay beyond the stars. He had journeyed to Earth and crash-landed.

"Is that how you met him?" I asked from the chair next to Aisha. Her hand took mine, and I immediately felt a brief rush of comfort.

"Yes," Pythia said. Her chair, which resembled a motorized wheel-chair, now hovered in the air. "He dragged himself from the wreckage of his ship, and I brought him home and sheltered him. When he told me why he was here, I was just as stunned and scared as you must be now.

"I realized, however, if he was telling the truth and I didn't help him, it would only be a matter of time before the Wraiths came to our planet." She rotated the chair to face a slowly-turning hologram of the galaxy. "So, I helped him build this lab, and this is where the Cybersuits were built." She looked around her. "This is also where he built me this chair."

"By Allah, this is unbelievable," Aisha muttered, and I squeezed her hand.

Gavin's mother turned her attention back to us. "I'm sorry to say this is as real as it gets." She then pressed a few buttons on the projector and a rotating hologram of Earth zoomed in. "Now the Wraiths are invading our planet. Not a soul on Earth can hide from them, and they won't stop until every man, woman, and child is under their control."

Her concern was as clear as the lines on her face, and she paused as if her next words were almost too heavy to release. "Right now, the only thing standing between the Wraiths and their goal of enslaving the entire human race," she gave another long pause, "is you."

Blinking rapidly, I looked from her to the stunned faces around me. "What is that supposed to mean?" I demanded.

She turned her hard gaze on me. "I mean the second you allowed those suits to encase you, you were drafted into this war."

"Hold on, time out!" Hunter said, making the signal with his hands. "I don't know about the rest of you, but I don't remember meeting any recruiting officers tonight."

Sighing, she looked at us in turn. "You see, Shurgal crashed-landed to Earth again earlier today, and the Cybersuits you found came from his ship. I hoped to recover the them before your DNA was encoded, but unfortunately that didn't happen."

For a second, all of us sat in shocked silence.

"You're joking, right?" I finally asked.

"I wish I were," she answered.

"But..." I stammered while looking at the others, trying to find the right words, "we're just teenagers. How are we supposed to stop something that's already consumed other worlds? Couldn't you get—"

"Look," Pythia yelled, and I jumped as she pointed a finger at me, "the second you climbed into the Cybersuits, they were keyed to your DNA, which means they can't be used by anyone else! I'd hoped to find qualified people to fight the coming storm, but I don't have the codes to wipe the DNA key lock, and we don't have spare Cybersuits. It's you or no one."

When she finished, Gavin reappeared, his wings shifting with his movements. "Did you get hold of their parents?" she asked, turning her chair to face him.

He nodded. "Yes, I did. I told them they're here because they helped me get home to help you after a bad episode," he said as her head dropped and she frowned. "As it's so late, they agreed to let them spend the night. Also, your parents, your parents, and your parents," he looked at me, Aisha, and Hunter, "told me to tell you Mr. Plumber told them what happened and you're grounded."

We all groaned.

CHAPTER 10

SLAVE LABOR

Ian

I woke up late the next day in my favorite chair, the bottle finished and the glass still in my hand. I placed it on the coffee table and sat up, rubbing my eyes in an attempt to wipe the sleep from them. I heard a knock on my door, which sounded as loud as the bells of Notre Dame or the bell of King Seongdeok to me.

"Come in," I moaned. Casey opened the door and sighed at the empty bottle. "I'm in no mood for a lecture." I stood and went to the kitchen to splash water on my face, hoping it would help relieve my hangover.

I heard him turn to leave, but he stopped at the door. "Neither Terra nor Shurgal would want this for you. And I'm saying what a brother even if I'm only a half-brother should. If you keep this up, you'll kill yourself," he said before he left.

A mix of experience and mediation brought the throbbing in my head under some control, and I left my room. As soon I entered the control room, people jumped up, snapping to attention and giving me various salutes. After saluting back, I went to a console in the center of the room where Casey, Jen, and Elise stood.

"How are you feeling?" Casey asked.

"Virtually normal," I answered. As Damon joined us, we all went to a side conference room occupied by a round table. After everyone had taken a seat, I turned to Elise. "Did the wheelchair reveal any information?"

She nodded and moved her hands over the console buttons, and a floating hologram appeared.

"According to the serial number, it was purchased by the state, and according to the records of Health and Human Services and Social Services, it was given to one Blair Holmes." An image of the girl's face appeared on the screen. "She was placed in foster care when her mother was killed in a vehicular benzene fire about a year ago."

"The mother?" I asked.

"Joan Holmes," she said. "Aside from a social security number, birth certificate, and death certificate, we can't find anything on her—not even a photo."

"That's odd in this day and age." I frowned.

She shrugged. "Either she was extremely camera shy, she was hiding from something or someone, or the records were completely wiped around the time she died—or before."

I thought for a moment as I bit my lip. "It would take a heck of a virus to wipe all of that from the human internet," I said, taking a moment to review the rotating face of the girl named Blair. "Only U.S. Marshals and other federal agencies around the globe have access to them."

"That doesn't make sense," Casey said. "If you're suggesting the woman went into a version of witness protection, why not take her daughter with her?"

"Maybe she tried," Jen offered. "Maybe Blair got pulled by the wrong people and Joan's waiting to make contact."

Slowly, I nodded. "It's possible. Once you're in the program, they'll let you contact family only once it's safe for you and them." I glanced once more at the image of the teen. "We'll have to look into that later. Right now, we have to find her and whoever else was with her before the Wraiths do." I pressed a few console buttons, and at once the image of the teen shifted to the side and Doc's face appeared.

"Commander," Doc said with a nod.

"How's Shurgal?" I asked.

Her eyes shifted nervously. "Ian, I did all I could."

I felt the blood drain from my face. "Doc, is he…" I couldn't form the word.

"He's alive," she reassured me, and I sighed in relief, "but he's in a coma." I froze. "I don't know if he can or will ever wake up."

Before I could say anything, the commlink sounded, indicating a call coming in. "Yes," I answered as Karl's head appeared next to Doc's.

"Ian, we have a problem," Karl said, and I turned my chair to look at him.

"What?"

"There are too many fail-safes built into the suit."

"We knew that before we retrieved it," I said with a wave of my hand. "What's wrong?"

"What's wrong is that, if we get the reset code wrong even once, it will detonate."Groaning in frustration, I lowered my eyes and ran my fingers through my hair. "We scanned it, which prompted a detonation warning. Ian, if we try to run diagnostics in any way, aside from repairs, the suit will self-destruct."

"Which means we can't mass produce them," Damon said.

"Shurgal did his job well," I said, looking back up at everyone. "He made it practically impossible for the Wraiths to learn anything from the suits if they fell into the wrong hands. If the prototype had the same security measures, Kizor wouldn't risk losing their only Cybersuit. This also means we're in big trouble," I finished, leaning my face into the palms of my hands.

At once, I felt all their eyes on me. "What do you mean?" Julies asked the question they all were thinking.

"It means I have to go out into the field if we want to use that suit."

"Ian, you can't!" Casey said. "We need you here! Without you, this place would fall apart!"

"It's more than that," Elise said. "Kizor probably built a reputation on killing you. If he finds out you're alive—"

"He'll do everything he can to make sure nobody finds out," I finished for her. "We don't have a choice. That suit is keyed to my DNA and mine alone. If I don't go, it's nothing more than an advanced paperweight!" For a second, I held their gazes before they slowly lowered theirs, knowing I was right.

I leaned back in my chair, resting my chin in one hand. "Do we know what school Blair goes to?" Elise nodded. "Do we have any contacts there?"

"Yes, two," Casey said.

"Get in touch with them. I want to know who could have been with the girl last night in the salvage yard. If we find them, we find the suits!"

Alec

The next morning, Hunter and I headed toward the kitchen after taking turns in one of the upstairs bathrooms. There was no sign of Aisha or Blair.

"So, what do you think—" Hunter frozen as we passed through the kitchen door.

Before us stood Gavin, a box of cereal in one hand and a full bowl in the other. He was bare from the waist up, except for the pair of leather straps buckled across his well-toned chest and abdomen that bound his wings to his back.

"Well, that certainly explains your hunched back and why you never took off that long coat," Hunter said, moving forward to circle him. "And there I was, hoping what happened last night was a nightmare."

"Sorry to disappoint," Gavin said, putting the cereal down on the counter. "I can't exactly go around town looking like an angel—the Catholics would probably put me on display."

I moved forward, my eyes locked on his wings. "Isn't that uncomfortable?" I asked, reaching out to touch a wing but stopping just short of contact.

"You get used to it," he said, taking a spoon from a drawer. He then added, "Just get it over with."

"Huh?"

"I know you want to touch them, so get it over with," he clarified.

I reached forward and gently placed my hand on top of the feathered joint of a wing. The feathers were surprisingly soft, and the powerful flight muscles flexed beneath them.

"Can you feel that?" I asked in wonder as another question came to mind. "How did you get your suit last night?"

"Yes," Gavin said simply, turning so my hand slipped from his wing, "and my mother called me to say she'd detected their locator beacons. We followed them to the closest one—the rest is history. She wasn't happy when I climbed in, though." I nodded at his story.

"Must be murder taking a shower with those, huh?" Hunter asked, his eyes shifting up and down.

"Not really." Gavin turned to face us. "It's better than having to stand in the rain to wash them."

"Where are Aisha and Blair?" I asked, looking around.

"Aisha is outside, doing her morning prayers," Gavin said with a nod of his head. "She's been out there for a while."

Just then, Pythia came into the kitchen on her crutches with Blair rolling beside her in a borrowed wheelchair. "When Shurgal and I built the Cybersuits," she began, "we never could have dreamed it would one day give someone the chance to see for the first time in her life." She shuffled to the table and sat down.

"By Allah, I will always be grateful," Aisha said as she came in through the sliding glass door. Smiling, she maneuvered through the room to the table, following the rhythmic tapping of her cane, and I helped her take a seat.

"It must have happened through the neural connection controls," Gavin's mother speculated.

"Neural connection?" I asked.

"It's how you were able to move the suits as you would your own bodies," she explained. "The suits connected to the neuro outputs of your brains and directly fed data into them to maximize response times and for you to understand the readouts."

"Wait a minute," I said, holding up one hand as I pondered her words.

"Are you saying those things were downloading all that data into our brains?" She nodded. "What was all that stuff on the view screen, then?"

"There is no view screen," Pythia answered. "That was the input data connected to your sight nerves, so you saw what the suit saw in a way you would understand," she said as we looked at each other.

"I want you all to pay attention," she said seriously as she looked at each of us for a moment. "When you go to school today, you must give away *nothing* about what happened last night. Not only would your lives be in danger if word ever got back to the Wraiths, but also the lives of everyone in this room and everyone you know." We sent nervous looks around the table. "From now on, you can trust *no one* aside from the people in this room," she continued. "Not your family, not your friends, not your teachers—no one. *Anyone* could be possessed by a Wraith; from what the survivors of their invasions have told us, they are master impersonators and have access to every memory and instinct belonging to their hosts. One slip, no matter how small, could mean death—or worse—for all of us, and with it the enslavement of the human race."

Silence fell, but then she turned toward her son and said, "for that reason, I don't think you should go back to school. It was risky before, but…"

"I understand, Mom," Gavin said, unbuckling the straps on his chest. "Back to homeschooling."

"I'll drive the rest of you to school." She rose to her feet with the help of her crutches. "You need to figure out a way to return here tonight— we still have much to discuss."

Ian

Half a block from the school, I sat on my Kawasaki Ninja, my back to the building. I was dressed in a black leather jacket and pants, and my helmet visor was tinted, concealing my face.

Through one of my mirrors, I watched the school entrance. Students had been let out over an hour ago, but now a small group of kids walked over to a set of parents waiting to pick them up.

What the… I thought, surprised, upon seeing one girl with a cane. Surely this was the right group, though—one of the girls had a wheelchair.

"Are you all seeing what I'm seeing?" I asked the faces of my team, which were projected on the helmet visor.

"Yeah," Casey said, stunned.

"Is that girl blind?" Jen asked, eyes narrowing.

"That *can't* be them," Jules said, sounding just as surprised as the rest. "Didn't you say *all* the Cybersuits were escaping the Wraiths?"

"According to our contacts, it can't be anyone else," I said, continuing to watch them as I struggled to work out this puzzle. "The suits' neural connections must have somehow compensated for any abilities the kids are lacking," I finally suggested. "We'll have to ask Shurgal to confirm this when he regains consciousness. Personally, I find it rather fitting." The Wraiths eliminated any hosts they considered physically weak, but now the "defectives" would have a chance to strike against them. "I'm going to go see someone," I announced, pulling back into the traffic. Now that I had tracked down the kids, I had to plan my next move carefully. "I'll probably be out for a while."

Alec

I said goodbye to my friends and headed for my dad's car. When I opened the back door, I saw that Annabelle, my five-year-old sister, was buckled into her booster seat.

"Somebody's in trouble," she greeted me in a singsong voice.

"Annabelle," my mother warned, looking at us through the rearview mirror, "don't antagonize your brother."

"Accurate, though," my father said as he started the car.

"It wasn't my fault, Dad—"

"It never is," he interrupted, and my mother put a hand on his shoulder to calm him.

"I wasn't the one who hit Bradley—that was Blair!" I said. "I just defended her with Hunter and Aisha!"

"What about last night?" Dad snapped. "Why didn't you call us? Why did it have to be Gavin who called to say you were at his place?"

"My phone died," I answered, using the story we'd come up with on the way to school, "and they didn't have the right charger!"

"You still should have called us," he said angrily.

"I talked to Gavin's mother this morning," he continued, and I held his gaze in the mirror. "Since her episodes are coming more frequently, Gavin's been taken out of school to study at home, and they're going to need someone to do the yard and housework."

"You've gotta be kidding me..." I moaned.

"I'm not," he said. "I'm taking you to their house after dinner for your first shift of the month."

"Daddy," Annabelle asked, eagerness in her voice, "can Alec clean my room, too?"

He looked at her through the rearview mirror, and Mom turned in her seat.

"That would be a big no," I said, shooting her a smug smile at the small victory.

"Don't push it, Alec!" Dad warned. "We're going to continue this discussion when we get home."

CHAPTER 11

TRAINING BEGINS

Alec

That night, I stood in the curved driveway of Gavin's giant log home, watching as my dad drove away. Sighing, I climbed the stairs next to the ramp and stood before the front door, which was framed by log pillars. As I reached for the bell, the door opened with Hunter on the other side.

"So, how long did your parents lecture you?" he asked, crossing his arms and leaning against the frame.

"It seemed like forever," I answered, stepping inside, "but it was probably only a couple of hours."

"Is that Alec?" Gavin's mother called from the other room. Before I could answer, she came around the corner on her crutches. "Good, you're finally here. Let's get down to the lab." Pythia reversed directions.

"Hello to you, too," I murmured as we followed. "Looks like you found a reason for us to be here."

When we reached the kitchen, she opened the door to the basement. "I told you I would," she replied before settling into the lift chair along the wall. "Gavin and the girls are waiting for us downstairs."

"Does that mean we don't need to mow the lawn and do housework?" Hunter asked as we walked down the stairs behind her chair as it traveled down, accompanied by the whirl of a small motor.

"Of course not," she snapped. "Shurgal built me some robots to take care of most of that—after I was diagnosed with MS, he wanted to make sure I didn't have to worry about anything."

She reached the bottom and removed the safety harness, took up her crutches, and climbed from the chair.

"What are we going to be doing here, then?" I asked, looking around the seemingly normal basement, including a wall of neatly organized tools and a garden hose hanging from hooks. I then spotted the bank of high-end computers with multiple screens along the opposite wall.

"I'm a scientist," she explained as she followed my gaze, "not a soldier." She looked at me again. "I'll do everything I can, however, to make you the warriors the galaxy and beyond needs."

She turned toward the wall of tools, and we watched as she turned a large wrench until it was horizontal. She then flipped a hammer upon its head, moved to a saw, and turned it counterclockwise until the blade faced the other direction.

Looking at me, she instructed, "Go to the computer." At once, I moved over to the shut-down machine. "On the keypad, type 3, 18, 1, 26, 25, 8, 15, 18, 5."

When I punched in the last number, there was a hiss as part of the floor rose before splitting off to the side. What looked like a heavy-duty metal door slid open and a elevator large enough to hold us all rose.

We climbed in and were quickly lowered into a cave, where Aisha and Blair were waiting.

As the elevator stopped, Gavin soared down toward the ground from another part of the cave and landed with a few flaps of his wings.

"I don't know if I'll ever get used to that," Blair said in awe as he folded his wings closed.

"Did you have any problems with your parents?" I asked the group as I climbed out of the elevator.

"They took my phone," Aisha said, turning toward the sound of my voice.

"Grounded for a month," Hunter said behind me.

"Didn't even bat an eye," Blair answered, maneuvering her borrowed chair toward us. She then turned to Pythia. "So, what's going to happen here?"

The woman shifted to her hover chair and said, "I will prepare you to the best of my abilities. Follow me."

After sharing a look Hunter and I followed with Blair guiding Aisha in the right direction.

Pythia pressed a few buttons on her chair, and with another hiss, sections of the floor opened in a circular pattern. Closed tubes rose from them before stopping and opening, revealing the suits.

"Get in," she said before pressing another button and lighting up a wide, empty section of the cave.

"We used it mainly to test the suits' weapons and targeting systems," she said, answering my unasked question. "Now they're going to show me how well you can shoot."

Ian

That night, I sat across the street from the gated driveway of a large, two-story log cabin style mansion, still on my motorcycle. At first glance, it looked very normal.

"If you don't look carefully enough, you'd miss that the place is practically a fortress," Casey said over the commlink.

I nodded as I eyed the solar panels and wind turbine on the roof. "I bet it could be taken completely off the grid, if it isn't already, and it would be difficult to sneak up on," I murmured as the screen zoomed in on the various cameras and a sensor scan revealed the windows were bulletproof.

"Who lives here?" I asked.

"A computer scientist who hit it big about fourteen years ago," Jen answered as her holographic face reviewed data I couldn't see.

"How?" I asked.

"You know those robotic vacuums that appeared a couple years ago?" Jen asked, her gaze returning to me, and I nodded. "She was one of the key programmers and designers for most of the early models.

She's become somewhat of a hermit in the last decade," Elise said. "She hardly leaves her property, except for doctor's visits—"

"Doctor's visits?" I interrupted.

"It appears that, about thirteen years ago, she was diagnosed with multiple sclerosis," Elise continued, annoyed at my interruption as she frowned face tightening. "We learned from her medical records that she's confined to a wheelchair or uses crutches."

"Family?" I inquired.

"She's an only child," Jen read. "Her parents, also loaded, died when their sailing yacht went down..." She fell silent, her face going pale.

"What?" I pressed. "What happened?"

"According to the Coast Guard report," she continued, "the people who built the yacht cut corners. When the family took the boat out a week after they'd bought it, a leak sprung in the engine room. They'd turned toward land but they didn't make it; the Coast Guard found what was left of the yacht hung up on a reef not far from shore with only the masts poking out of the water. Their six-month-old baby was secured to the top of the highest mast."

At the end of the story, I closed my eyes in sorrow. "She must be afraid of the water now from the stories of what happened?"

"Not that I can tell. According to what I'm seeing, she owns a few boats, herself, including a two-hundred-foot motor yacht moored on the coast.

"Her only living family is her son, Gavin, born about thirteen years ago."

"And?" I prompted when she remained silent.

"That's it," she said, looking at me in surprise. "According to the records we have, he was born at home and was homeschooled until a few years ago. He was unenrolled from the same high school as the other teens yesterday."

I frowned in thought, but before I could comment, the faces of Damon and Jules appeared.

"Ian, you better get back here," Damon said urgently.

"What is it?" I asked.

"It's the prisoners," Damon said. "Something's happening, and we think you should be here."

"I'm on my way," I said before discreetly leaving my hiding spot. When I was a safe distance away, I gunned the engine.

Back in El Dorado, Klaus and Damon met me in the hangar. I swung my leg off my motorcycle and approached them.

"Updates," I snapped after I removed my helmet.

"It might be better to see for yourself," Klaus said. We entered a maglift, and a couple seconds later, the lift door opened. Walking quickly down the hall, we came to two armored doors with room for another heavier pair to seal the room shut. With a hiss, the doors opened, and we walked into the brig.

Reaching the force field–sealed cell, I saw the man and woman I had captured on the floor of their cells. Tiny beads of sweat covered their foreheads.

I looked at Casey, who waited with Elise, Jen, and Doc. "What's happening to them?"

Doc shrugged. "I've never encountered anything like this," she said, bewildered. "The scans I just took indicate fluctuations in their brain activity, as well as their vitals."

As I considered that, I studied the slumped pair. "Did you take care of those orders I gave this morning?" I muttered to Casey, and he nodded and whispered into my ear.

Making a decision, I picked up a security clearance badge that would allow me to enter the cell and pinned it to my chest before I walked into the cell. They looked up at me as I pressed a button on the wall and a chair slid out, along with today's paper. I sat down and opened it to the sports section, wondering about Anaheim's chances at the cup.

After a moment, the man said, "What do you want, Centaurien?"

I looked at him out of the corner of my eye. "What do you think I want, Wraith? Information."

"What makes you think we're going to give you any?" the woman scoffed.

I folded the paper in half, scanning an article in the hockey section. "The pair of you don't look so good," I said, keeping my eyes on the news.

They turned away from me and gave a visible pang of agony. I set the paper aside. "If you don't talk to us, how can we help you?"

They glared at me, and the man growled, "It doesn't matter."

I glanced at my team outside the cells before looking back at the couple before me. "What do you mean?" I asked, and they stared at me.

They looked at each other and then back at me. "Because we'll be dead before you can do anything," the woman finally said in a weakened voice.

Before I could ask what she meant, their eyes flashed and they began to convulse. I jumped back through the force field as the pair arched their backs. When their faces came into view, I stared at their silent screams of agony.

"I need med teams to the brig *now*!" Doc yelled into a communicator.

For a moment, the pair continued to convulse, but then they suddenly stopped, their bodies arched in a bridge as they balanced on their heads and feet.

The med teams burst in.

"No, wait!" I held out an arm to block them.

"Ian, you can't!" Doc objected.

"Look!" I pointed.

Before us, the faces of the man and woman shifted and began to rapidly flash. They exhaled deeply, and what looked like a gassy cloud rose from each of them. They collapsed to the floor, breathing hard like they had just run a marathon.

The clouds seemed to hover before they moved toward the force field; we all instinctively jerked back but were grateful when the force field flashed, restricting the Wraiths to the cell.

For a second, the humans rose from the floor and hovered in the air, but then they rolled over and dragged themselves away from the floating clouds, which I felt were somehow watching us.

I then saw what looked like fine dust drop beneath the clouds like falling rain. More and more fell until all that was left was a fine layer of particles on the floor. For a moment, all I could do was stare at the small piles of dust that had been Wraiths seconds before. Slowly, I moved forward and dropped to one knee to run the tips of my fingers through their remains.

"What just happened?" I asked the man and woman now looking up at us.

"They're dead," the woman answered, still breathing heavily. "They... they starved to death. Wraiths need to go back to their base to feed, but you locked them up here."

Before I could say more, they suddenly enveloped me in their arms. "Thank you," they both said at once as they started to sob.

"Thank you for giving us our lives back," the man said as he pulled back, tears running down his face.

Alec

The next day, Dad dropped me off at school, and I waved goodbye to him. The majority of the arriving students mingled in groups as they moved toward the two-story building.

I froze as the events of the last few days hit me like a ton of bricks. If everything I'd learned was true, then anyone—*anyone*—could be possessed by a Wraith and we wouldn't know until it was too late. The whole planet was in serious trouble. One wrong move and we'd be finished.

"Alec?" When I whipped around, Hunter stepped back, hands raised. "Whoa! Easy, there," he said.

I shook my head and then turned to look up at the school. "Sorry—I've just got a lot on my mind."

Patting my shoulder, Hunter said, "Me too."

I nodded as we made our way to our lockers. As I spotted Blair and Aisha, I quickly averted my gaze stopping Hunter from waving at them as I did.

"What are you doing?" Hunter asked in a low voice, and I glanced at his frown. "Why are you ignoring them?"

Biting my lip and glancing around to make sure no one was eavesdropping, I murmured, "To avoid drawing attention to us."

After a second, he shrugged. "I see your point, but wouldn't it be better for people to get used to us being a group as soon as possible?" Arching his eyebrows, he moved toward Blair and Aisha.

As I watched him go, I realized he was right. *We just might be able to become a team, after all.* I slung my bag over my shoulder and followed him.

"It's nice to see you outside of our holding cell," Hunter said as he reached the pair. "Did you get that oil problem fixed, Blair?"

Sighing, I closed my eyes in exasperation, and Blair gave him a hard sideways look. "Do you want me to crush your feet under my wheels?"

"Miss Holmes!" a hard voice growled, and we turned to see Mr. Plumber's cold stare. "I see you still need to work on that temper. I want you all in my office at the end of last period." He turned and walked away.

"Does anyone else have a chill running down their spine?" Hunter asked. Before I could reply, however, the first-period bell rang out.

CHAPTER 12
NEW ARRANGEMENTS

Alec

For the rest of the school day, my thoughts fluctuated between the potential fate of the planet and the more immediate problem of Plumber. Had he concocted some new kind of punishment? Did he have new charges against us?

At that last thought, I sighed, rolling my eyes. *Come on, Alec,* I thought. *Stop working yourself up into a frenzy. Right now, there's nothing you can do.*

Still, I couldn't keep my eyes from wandering to the groups of fellow classmates around me. My mind raced at the thought that I might be surrounded by an enemy—one that could mean a fate worse than death if they ever managed to get to me or my friends. How many would rather die than meet that fate?

"Alec?" I felt a light shove on my shoulder, which sent my thoughts crashing back to Earth.

With a jerk, I blinked. Glancing around, I saw that everyone had turned their attention toward me. In front of me, I saw my English teacher, open book in hand, staring at me with an exasperated look.

"It's nice to see your head's out of the clouds," he said, moving back to lean against his desk. "Perhaps you can display the merits of your method of paying attention." He fixed me with a hard look. "Could you tell me significance of the scene in Hamlet after he sprung his test and—"

"It's the part of the play that holds the fate of all the characters," I said, interrupting him. "It was the most significant turning point and rested solely on the choices he made. Because of those choices, not only did Hamlet pay the price, but so did all the people he cared for."

My teacher blinked in surprise. "Very good, Alec—" he started to say, but I interrupted him again.

"It could also serve as an example of—"

"That will do, Alec," he said insistently, looking at me with a frown. "You may go back to daydreaming."

As he turned back to the whiteboard, everyone snickered and Hunter shook with laughter, barely able to contain himself.

Later, we gathered outside Mr. Plumber's office. Aisha sat beside me, her cane folded on her lap, and Blair sat on the other side in her borrowed chair. Across from us, Hunter leaned against the wall, arms crossed over his chest. Mr. Plumber's door was closed, which seemed like an ominous sign.

I glanced at the secretary, who continued to type at her computer, ignoring us, and then I glanced again at Mr. Plumber's door. "So, what do you think?" I looked at Hunter.

"Is he trying to sweat us out—trying to see which one of us will break first?" he asked.

"Actually, Hunter," we all turned to see the vice principal standing in the doorway, "I have better ways to break people than that." He gave us a hard look. "Now, if you would all step inside...." He waved his hand toward his desk.

We followed him in and he sat on his high-backed desk chair as if it were a throne. "After a meeting with your parents and Mr. Kelly," he growled, sounding like something was stuck in his throat, "it has been decided—against my better judgment—that your detentions have been lifted." I heard my friends release sighs of relief as I did the same. "However," he added, and we all froze, "instead, you will all be enrolled at once at either of the martial arts academies: Black Tiger or Golden Dragon. Tomorrow and the day after, you will report to each school so we can determine which is the better fit for you."

I raised my eyebrows and saw that my friends looked shocked.

"Blair," he added, and we braced for his next words, "something was dropped off for you this morning at the front doors. You will need to see one of the school officers for it." He then dismissed us with a wave of his hand.

Outside the office, we let loose noisy sighs of relief. I shrugged and said, "Well, at least we're out of detention."

"Yeah," Blair nodded, "but I have no idea who would have left something for me here." She turned toward Officer Hernandez's office and we followed. "Maybe it's my foster parents' idea of a sick joke." When we arrived, Blair turned her borrowed chair sideways to knock on the door.

"Enter!"

Before we could move to help her, she maneuvered her chair, opened the door, and slipped inside; I barely caught the door before it closed behind her and we followed in her wake.

"Officer Hernandez, I was told that—" Blair froze midsentence. The reason was obvious: her own wheelchair was there, waiting for her.

"This was left for you at the front door," Officer Hernandez said from behind her desk with a wave of her pen, "and this was attached to it." She held out a sealed envelope.

"Thanks."

When we returned to the hall, Blair ripped open the envelope and took out a folded piece of paper. Peering over her shoulder, I saw that it contained just two words with a name and a phone number beneath them:

Let's talk.

CHAPTER 13

GOLDEN DRAGON

Ian

For most of the night I sat, my eyes on the untraceable cell phone on a small table which had refused to ring the whole night.

The next morning, I walked down the hall, swinging into my jacket and getting ready to go out for the day. As I returned salutes from people I met on the way, Karl dashed to me in the hallway near the ground vehicle hangar.

"Commander!" he waved one hand.

"Karl," I sighed, smiling, as the doors hissed opened and walked into the hangar, "I think, after all this time, you can just call me Ian." He regarded me with a stern look. Sighing again, I rolled my eyes. "What is it?"

"I wanted to give you these before you headed out," he said, holding up a pair of black sport sunglasses. Frowning, I plucked them from his hand and closely examined them.

"Uh, sorry to tell you this, buddy, but sunglasses have been around for almost a hundred years," I said, shaking them.

"Not like these," he answered. "Over the last couple of days, I've been looking over the sensor you told us about when you acquired the Cybersuit. This is only a prototype, but it could help in the war to come."

I looked at the glasses again. "Well, if they mean so much to you," I said, flipping them open and slipping them on. At once, I noticed a minuscule dot of light on the lenses, and then readouts and a list of modes appeared. "Okay, not much of a difference," I said, reading through them. "It's still got the standard night vision, x-ray, infrared, uplink, and rear camera... but what's PM 8?"

"Prototype mode 8," he answered. "When you get the chance to test it out, you'll know what it's for." With that, he turned and left.

Alec

After school, we were picked up by a shuttle bus and taken to Golden Dragon Martial Arts Academy. I took a seat next to Hunter while Blair locked the brakes of her chair and sat beside Aisha, whose red hijab bobbed lightly to the music she listened to in one ear. I sat quietly, absorbed in my thoughts, and about ten minutes later, the shuttle came a stop, the airbrakes whistling, outside Golden Dragon.

The building looked like it had been repurposed from a warehouse. Above the doors, an old sign adorned the side of the building with a golden dragon on one side and a tiger climbing a series of rocks on the other, the two animals chasing each other in a yin and yang design.

I pressed the handicap button for Blair, who had wheeled up the ramp, and as the double doors swung open, we all filed in.

Before us was a large, open area, the floor covered with thick mats with a series of large sparring circles. Along the walls hung a few lines of standing heavy bags and hanging heavy punching bags, and a large mirror ran along the far wall. A boxing ring was set up in the middle of the room, and in a corner were a trampoline and gymnastics equipment. There was a corner window next to a weight room, as well as a tall rock and bouldering wall.

"You must be the hopeful new students," said a kind voice, and we looked over at the smiling face of a gentle-looking, young Asian woman behind a desk. Her long, black hair was tied back in a ponytail, and she stood and walked toward us in a martial arts uniform. "It's nice to meet you. I'm Tora Yamato." We each shook her offered hand.

"My grandfather runs the school, and I'm one of the many senseis," she explained. "If you'll follow me, I'll show you our facilities."

"Uh, is it going to matter that Aisha and I have physical disabilities?" Blair asked as she wheeled her chair alongside Sensei Yamoto.

"Why would it?" a toned, muscular man with short, dirty-blond hair spoke as he approached wearing a gi. "We've had students who were either blind or partially blind," he said with a smile, "and a couple went on to become national champions. We've also had a student in a wheelchair before."

"This is Jason Walker," Sensei Yamato said. "If things work out for you here, he will be your teacher."

"Nice to meet you all," Sensei Walker nodded at each of us and shook our hands.

"Jason," Sensei Yamato said, "why don't you show the boys the men's lockers, while I show the girls? We'll meet up in the workout room."

Ian

After I showed Alec and Hunter the men's lockers, I led them to the workout room, where Blair and Aisha waited.

"So, why a weight room?" Alec asked as I opened the door.

"We think we should teach more than just how to kick and punch," I explained.

"And the rock wall?" Hunter asked, eyeing it and the dangling ropes.

Smiling, I moved toward him. "Rock climbing is more than scaling the next mountain," I said. "All climbers climb in pairs, and more often than not, it's about trust."

Frowning, they looked up at the rock and bouldering wall. "So you took a hobby and turned it into a trust exercise?" Alec asked, and I nodded.

I then showed them the gymnastics section of the academy, explaining that it was used mainly to improve students' flexibility, agility, and balance. I also clarified that one side of the academy was used by kids and the other by teens and adults but the ring could be used by everyone.

At the end of the tour, I opened a rear door and led them into a smaller version of the room we had just left. "This is where we do our private classes. You'll find most of the same equipment here, and you are also free to use the weight and wall room and the other equipment, plus the ring." They eyed the hanging bags, Wavemasters, and wall mirrors.

"It's really no issue that Aisha and I have physical problems?" Blair asked again.

"Of course not," I reassured her. "You see, we train a hybrid system here, incorporating aspects of judo, a throwing style, aikido, a flow-and-misdirect style, and jui jitsu, a gentle but devastating joint manipulation style. Kickboxing, muay Thai, krav maga, jeet kune do, taekwondo, karate, and kung fu are all striking styles. We take aspects from each in a blend, like other hybrid styles, such as ninjutsu and pankration.

"Blair, your strengths will be in throwing and joint manipulation. Aisha, you can work with every system—when one sense is limited, the others pick up the slack. I'm sure we can awaken your inner daredevil."

Alec

Blair and Aisha changed in the women's locker rooms as Hunter and I changed into the uniforms we had been given in the men's.

"So, what do you think?" I asked, adjusting my gi top.

"They sure seem to know their stuff," Hunter said, tying the side tabs of his top in place, "and they seem to care about their students." After securing the white belt, he started making high-pitched sounds and chopping hand movements; he spun around, pretending to throw a punch to close the locker, but his hand froze less than an inch from the open metal door, and he then closed it with one finger.

We entered the private classroom in the back to find Aisha and Blair similarly dressed, although Aisha still wore her red hijab. In front of the classroom stood Sensei Walker, who motioned for us to line up next to the girls.

"As I was saying, Blair, you will be focusing primarily on hand strikes. Later, if everything works out with you and the school, we'll include throws and grappling. Aisha, Sensei Yamato will help you create the right postures and forms." Aisha nodded. "Yoi!" he called suddenly, snapping to attention. "Sensei ni rei!"

We followed suit, and as Sensei Yamato bowed, we did the same.

Ian

An hour and a half later, the class was finished. After the teens had changed, Tora and I watched them pass through the glass doors.

"So, that was them," she said.

"Hmm," I nodded.

"I met them, but I still can't believe it." Her voice was filled with awe. "One blind and one confined to a wheelchair, not to mention they're all so young…."

"I seem to remember a time when your grandfather said the same thing about you," I grinned, jabbing my thumb at an old framed photo of previous senseis. Tora's grandfather, whom I had fought beside in World War II after my plane was shot down, had won the Medal of Honor before he went on to found the school.

"Grandfather always said it was his greatest honor to have been your friend."

"The honor was mine," I replied as I headed toward the men's locker room.

"Do you think they'll choose this school?" Tora asked from the door while I changed.

"Well, our contact at their high school said he would encourage them to join us," I answered, stepping into my jeans.

"What if they don't?" she asked as I came out, pulling on my duster.

"We'll cross that line when we get to it," I reassured her. "Tomorrow, they'll try out Black Tiger, and I'll be close by to keep an eye on them."

CHAPTER 14

BLACK TIGER

Alec

With Hunter beside me in our Cybersuits, I ran, arms pumping, down an alley with blank walls on either side. Glancing over my shoulder, I saw another one of the Zorvains behind us.

"See anything?" Hunter asked.

"Just the couple hundred Zorvains chasing us!" I snapped at him.

Before he could reply, something snagged my leg, and I went down hard. Rolling onto my back, I stared in horror as what looked like part of the ground reached up and grabbed me by the ankle. The blood drained from my face as I watched a section of the ground shift and expand until what looked like living slime glared back at me with black eyes. Its arm extended to keep its grip on me as it slowly stood.

A metal bar suddenly almost cut it in half, but before Hunter could pull it free, the creature grasped it with both hands, and a slimy foot shot out, kicking him in the chest and sending him hurtling into a wall.

I watched as the creature drew itself back together, pulling the bar through its body until it popped out the other side. As Hunter stepped toward the creature again, it swung the bar at him hard.

He raised one arm to block it, and it snapped in two. Hunter immediately seized the creature and threw it, face first, into the wall. My eyes widened as I watched what had been the front of the creature grow out of the back.

Hunter reacted by throwing a punch at the creature's face. As the ooze caved, it encased his hand and formed into a pair of hands, grasping his fist. The creature's head reappeared, then, and it spun around, throwing Hunter against the wall.

Desperate to help my friend, my eyes darted everywhere for a weapon. Suddenly, with a screech, the wall in front of me crashed down on my attacker. I watched as the slimy substance oozed from underneath the pile and looked up to see Gavin hovering in the air above.

"Simulation terminated!" Pythia's voice said over the intercom, and the world around us dissolved in flashing octagonal patterns once more revealing the cave.

"Gavin," I snapped as he lowered himself to the ground, "what was that all about?"

"I guess I got tired of seeing you two running," he replied.

"That was not your call!" I jabbed my armored finger into his chest. "We had a plan!"

"And what was that," he asked, "running for your life?"

"Gavin!" his mother's voice snapped over the intercom, and we all looked up at where she manned the computers on a rocky over hang with Blair and Aisha looking over her shoulder. "The next one's yours. Now get back up here!"

After sending us a look we couldn't see through the face plate, Gavin flew up to do as he was told.

"Alec, Hunter," we looked up at her, "you're not going to find more room in this simulation, so think of something else," she said as the environment we had been in reappeared. "Let's begin!"

"So, what's the plan this time?" Hunter asked as the Zorvains appeared before us.

"Bottleneck them!" I shifted my forearm to a cannon and opened fire.

When we were done for the night, Dad picked me up and I arrived home tired, moaning to myself over the targets I had missed after the simulation.

In the living room, Annabelle and Mom sat on the sofa, watching a movie with animated, singing and dancing characters.

"How was the slave labor?" Annabelle asked, a big grin on her face. "Get a lot of chores done for Gavin's mom?"

"Annabelle," Mom warned, pulling her back down onto the sofa.

"What?" she asked innocently.

I turned to my dad and said, playing the part, "Do I really have to keep doing this? I don't have to go to detention, anymore." He scowled at me. "So... that would be a yes," I moaned, falling into the armchair next to the sofa.

"Just be glad you don't have to be at your sister's beck and call," Dad said, moving in front of me and motioning me out of his favorite chair.

Moaning a second time, I pulled myself up and dropped onto the sofa beside Annabelle.

"its time for bed honey," Mom said coming out of the kitchen.

"aww Mom," Annabelle whined as Dad leaned toward the coffee table, snatched the remote, and changed the channel.

"Hey!" Annabelle complained.

"Sorry, honey. Game's on," he replied.

Annabelle pouted, her arms crossed. "We'll have to start it all over again," she whined.

"I know, honey," Mom said, patting her shoulder though I saw her eyes flash to the ceiling. As if she was hoping she would forget.

Looking up at me, Annabelle asked, "I heard you're going to tour Black Tiger?" I nodded. Smiling, she moved closer. "I have class tomorrow," she said slyly. "I guess, either way, I get to—"

Before she could finish, I put her in a headlock and gave her a noogie. "Just remember who's bigger than you," I said playfully as she begged for mercy. When I let her go, she smiled up at me and snuggled close.

After carrying her up to bed to tuck her in, my mind drifted to the world I had fallen into and the danger it meant for my family.

*

The next day, we took a shuttle to Black Tiger Academy. Hunter sat next to me. "Do you think we're going to see many differences from Golden Dragon? I'm not sure they can top what we saw yesterday—they were very accommodating with Blair and Aisha. Heck, they even had another student in a wheelchair give a demonstration!"

"Blair seemed convinced," I said, looking out the window.

"What did your parents say when you told them about Golden Dragon?" Hunter asked.

"They seemed excited. Annabelle was excited about me coming today," I answered.

"I forgot about that," he said. "She goes to Black Tiger, right?"

"For the last couple of years, yeah," I said. "She's a blue belt now."

"Well, maybe she can get you a family discount."

As the shuttle pulled into the parking lot, I looked out the window at the imposing building, which had been built a couple years ago next to the largest lake in the state. It was larger than Golden Dragon and resembled an old hangar with a curved roof. Behind it, the lake stretched, surrounded by forest, with the mountains in the distance.

After the shuttle came to a stop, Aisha, Hunter, and I climbed out before the chair lift was activated.

"How does it look?" Aisha asked.

When we were inside, we eyed the visible training rooms, which were very similar to those at Golden Dragon, but we didn't see a boxing ring, gymnastic area, or workout room.

"You must be the kids your school told us about." We all turned toward a well-muscled man in a gi.

"Alec!" Annabelle stood with the rest of the children's class Mom had dropped her off for, waving at me with a big smile on her face.

"Annabelle, eyes on your teacher!" the man before us reprimanded her. After one more wave to me, she turned back.

"So, you're the famous Alec," the man said, smiling, as he approached me. "I'm Sensei Clarkson, head instructor." He shook hands with each of us. "Please come this way; I will show you our facilities. Here at Black

Tiger, we pride ourselves in catering to each student's needs, because each student is different."

"Does that mean our disabilities won't be a problem?" Aisha asked, her black hijab shifting with her movements.

"Of course not," Sensei Clarkson said.

My eyes roamed the area, taking everything in. "Is that where you give private lessons?" I asked, nodding toward a door on a far wall.

After glancing over, he shook his head. "No, that's where advanced students train."

"Why not out here?" Hunter asked, frowning.

"We teach our advanced students techniques that, for lack for a better word, are dangerous," he explained. "We like to think that teaching them in private removes the temptation for the less advanced students to copy and use the techniques before they're ready."

"And it adds a little mystery and incentive to keep the less advanced students coming," Hunter said before I could.

With a smile, Sensei Clarkson led us to the door. "A couple advanced students are practicing against multiple opponents now."

When he opened it, we saw a black belt bound at the wrists and surrounded by four other students: three black belts and one red belt. He threw two front kicks at the student in front and sent him to the mat before stepping back, bringing his arms forward with circular motions, and breaking the grip of the person behind him. After delivering a hard side kick to another student, he then delivered a hard strike to the one who'd restrained him. Both dropped to the floor. He blocked the punch the last student threw and his spinning kick knocked her down.

"Joon bi!" the instructor called out, and they all sprang to attention and formed a line.

I realized then that the student in the middle was Bradley, and I moved back quickly. "Impressive," I told Sensei Clarkson.

"Don't worry—he didn't see you." I lifted my eyebrows at him. "Mr. Kelly told us what happened, and we made it clear to Bradley that it was settled," he explained. "He won't bother you again."

The sensei continued the tour around the facilities, explaining that, in order to reach the advanced training level, students needed to do community work. He also said the academy trained many law enforcement officers, both local and federal.

"Sometimes we even hold beach parties for the older students," he said, "since we are right on the water. We have a jet ski we let students use, as you well know, Alec with Annabelle going here."

Afterward, like at Golden Dragon, we went through a private class. All the instructors we worked with were exceptionally nice to us, and they took extra care when they worked with Blair and Aisha.

Finished with the class, Hunter and I changed back into our street clothes in the empty locker room. "What do you think?" I asked, slipping on my shirt.

"It's really nice," he replied. "The beach parties with the jet ski would be worth it." I chuckled, and then he said, "You'd be able to spend more time with Annabelle."

"Oh, like I need that," I scoffed, tying my shoes. "I'll go talk with Sensei Clarkson about possibly joining."

"Meet you out front!" he called as I walked through the door and a few students entered.

I saw no sign of Sensei Clarkson, so I made my ay to the back room, thinking he must have been there. I raised my hand to knock on the door but froze at the sound of voices inside.

"Blind and another crippled?"

"Tell me about it. Who would want one of them for a host?" I recognized Bradley's voice and frowned.

"No one—they're defective and should be eliminated."

"Soniss said the two boys are strong and would make good hosts. The other two would be good publicity—humans love that kind of stuff." This time, it was Sensei Clarkson's voice. I felt the blood drain from my face as I slowly backed away.

CHAPTER 15

NOT AMONG FRIENDS

Alec

I quickly walked down the aisle between the mats and joined my friends at the door.

"Did you talk to Sensei Clarkson?" Hunter asked as I approached.

"We've gotta go right now!" I hissed.

"Why? What's up?" Aisha asked, a frown forming on her face.

"We're not safe here," I whispered.

"So, what'd you guys think?" At the sound, I looked up in shock and turned to face Sensei Clarkson.

"We had a blast!" I said. *Make it convincing.* "But we've gotta go. In the evenings, we help out a woman with MS." I turned toward the door.

"MS?" Sensei Clarkson asked, following us out. "Well, that certainly counts as community work. Keep that up and you might become advanced students before you know it!"

"Thanks!" I said. "We'll let you know if we decide to come here."

We left him at the door and headed toward the shuttle. Just beyond it, a figure on a motorcycle wearing a duster was stopped at the side of the road. The tinted helmet screen obscured the rider's face.

"Alec," my mother said, cutting into my thoughts, "we've gotta go."

"Yes, Mom," I climbed into the front seat and buckled up.

"So, what do you think?" she asked as we pulled out.

"I think we'll be going to Golden Dragon."

"Aww," Anabelle whined behind me, "but I wanted you to go to Black Tiger with me!"

Looking at her in the rearview window I smiled at her. "well maybe you can transfer to Golden Dragon."

"Alec," Mom said, "you can go to Golden Dragon if you want, but after what happened, you know I'd like Anabelle to go to Black Tiger," she said.

Ian

Sitting on my bike down the road from Black Tiger, I watched the teens emerge from the academy.

"It looks like they're okay," Jen said in my ear.

"I'm not so sure," I murmured. "I can tell Alec's spooked."

Suddenly Karl's face appeared on the lower part of my visor. "Have you tested that new prototype mode?" he asked eagerly.

Sighing, I rolled my eyes. "No; I'm not even wearing the glasses right now."

"Well, just in case, I added it to your helmet visor, too," he said. "You could try it out now and see what has that kid spooked."

"Have I missed my quota for saying how obsessed you are?" I asked but reached up to open the small slot on the side of the helmet. Once I activated the new mode, the screen shimmered, and I froze. "Whoa..." I murmured.

"What do you see?" Karl asked eagerly.

"I'm not sure," I answered, eyeing the shimmering lights surrounding the instructor who had followed the teens out of the building. "One of the Black Tiger instructors has a shimmering aura."

"That's proof of what a genius Shurgal is!" Karl said excitedly.

"What are you talking about?"

"Every living being is surrounded by an electrical aura. Somehow, Shurgal isolated the frequency Wraiths produce—"

"And created a sensor to detect it," I finished for him with awe. "You found a way to make it visible."

Karl gave a smug smile. "Just a little reverse engineering and applying the right tech," he said, casually waving his discovery off.

"Let's make this standard issue as of yesterday," I said, glad we were gaining ground. The shuttle passed me, and I said, "I'd better get going before I draw attention to myself." I gunned the engine, made a tight U-turn, and drove off. "and Karl, next time tell me when you come up with something this good!"

"I didn't want to get hopes up only for them to be crushed."

Alec

When we gathered at Pythia's that evening, I leaned against one of the consoles as Blair and Aisha climbed back into their suits. I then told Pythia and Gavin everything I'd overheard.

"The Wraiths control Black Tiger," Gavin murmured, rubbing his chin as his wings shifted.

"Gavin," his mother said, "that's not proof that they are there—"

"Come on, Mom," Gavin faced her, his wings snapping open. "What Alec overheard is suspicious enough. They were talking like they were at a cattle auction and Aisha and Blair were diseased heifers."

Pythia was silent for a moment before she slowly nodded. "Okay. It sounds like we found them." She turned to Aisha and Blair. "What do you two think?"

"To be honest," Aisha said, "the teachers there kind of made my skin crawl."

"Same here," Blair said, "and there were times they were smiling that I swore I saw hate in their eyes. It was... freaky."

"Alec, what about you?" Lost in my thoughts, I didn't respond. "Alec?" Blinking, I shook my thoughts off and looked at Pythia. "Sorry. What?"

"What's got you so engrossed?" Hunter asked, shifting forward.

I glanced down before I looked up again. "Hamlet."

Hunter scanned the other confused faces before looking back at me. "What does Shakespeare have to do with anything?" he asked.

"Everything," I answered seriously. "Hamlet had the chance to end it and bring justice to his father, but he hesitated and everyone he loved paid the price." Hunter's frown deepened; Aisha nodded in understanding. "Well, I'm not going to make that mistake," I stated. "I have a little sister in that school, and she's in danger and doesn't know it. As her big brother, it's my job to protect and fight for her, and that's what I'm going to do." I turned to Pythia. "It's time we got serious. Can you increase the difficulty of the target practice?"

Pythia nodded with a grin. "I can make the targets smaller and increase their speed," she said, "and I can see if I can modify the stealth capabilities, as well. Also, if you think the other student, Bradley, is possessed, I might have something that will help us keep an eye on him."

She handed a small tracking device to Hunter. "He has a backpack, right? Sneak it into one of those tiny side pockets no one ever checks. When we meet again tomorrow, we'll review the data and see what he's been up to."

CHAPTER 16

YOUNG BUT STRONG

Ian

Holding my blasters on either side of my head, I rolled behind a pillar as blaster fire pierced my last hiding place. I waited a few seconds, and then I turned and fired the blasters at the advancing Zorvains. A few fell, bloody holes covering their chests.

I darted off to the side, firing as I went, and when I saw Sloozes coming at me, I holstered a blaster and grabbed an orb. After pressing a button and dropping the orb among the Sloozes, who fired at me, I rolled forward and ducked behind a crate, covering my head.

The explosion rocked the ground, and I heard the sickening sound of Slooze guts slap against the wall. Pieces of Slooze covered the backs of my hands, and I shook them vigorously. "Disgusting."

I then heard a sound and lifted my head to see a seven-foot-tall Zorvain pointing a blaster at me. After jumping up and sending two snap kicks that knocked the blaster from its hand, I launched myself, feet first, into its chest and felt its ribcage collapse under me.

I flipped and drew my blasters again, but suddenly twenty Zorvains surrounded me, weapons ready. I closed my eyes, knowing what was about to happen.

"Simulation terminated. Mission status: failed."

As the holograms disappeared, I holstered my blasters and the combat simulation dematerialized. Jen met me at the door and walked with me as I stormed down the hall, people saluting me as I went. As I barged into my rooms and stomped toward my bedroom, she took a seat on the sofa.

After shutting the door behind me, I threw my gear onto my bed, undressed quickly, and showered and changed. As I moved to the doorway with a towel wrapped around my neck, I saw Jen had picked up a holo-picture of Terra and me in combat training gear; we each had an arm over each other's shoulder, laughing at our success.

I closed my eyes, remembering that day—the day before she'd left. I slammed my fist into the doorframe and then plopped down on the other end of my sofa.

I rubbed my face with the towel. "Look, if you're going to say something, Jen, just say it."

She put the picture down. "Ian, there was time you could do that mission in your sleep, yet you failed it time and again today, like some rookie. What's on your mind? Is it Terra? Shurgal? Those teenagers?"

I looked away and said, "Maybe a little of all of the above."

She sighed. "Ian, maybe we should modify their memories of that night and make them forget it all."

My eyes snapped to her. "No, and I don't ever want to hear that suggestion again! We don't have a choice now, and you know that." I stood and walked over to lean on the mantel.

"Why? We have forces here."

"We aren't ready to protect the humans and ourselves with the few soldiers we have. If it were a contest of strength, who do you think would come out on top? Our resistance has to be done quietly. Thanks to the two I captured, we now know the location of one of their operation bases."

"And their weakness," Jen reminded, crossing her arms over her chest. "Once or twice a week, they have to leave their hosts to feed on particles collected in a mist from their home planet."

For a moment, I was silent. "I'm going to acquire some animal modes for combat. People in the field should be placed on constant yellow alert, and notify our human allies that they should be on guard. Advise them not to trust anyone and to be ready to come into the nearest base or outpost at a moment's notice."

"Yes, sir." She went to my door and pressed the release, but before she left, she asked, "Out of curiosity, what animals are you thinking of?"

"Some that I think will fit me," I said.

That night, wearing my Cybersuit, I crept along a jungle floor in Central Asia, keeping to the shadows. As I looked for my first stop, I crouched behind a bush and scanned the dark surroundings.

Come on, where are you? You come out at night to hunt, I thought. Then came the roar.

I spun around and saw my quarry sprinting at me through the darkness, his black and white pelt making him look like a ghost. I locked my eyes with his, and he took a few bounding steps before he slowed his pace. When he reached me, he gave a light roar and swatted the air between us. I didn't move, and my gaze didn't falter. Slowly, he gave a low moan as he sat back on his haunches and then dropped to his belly.

I took a breath as I gazed at the white Siberian tiger at my feet, admiring his beauty. I reached out and lightly ran my hand along his face, acquiring his DNA. As I pulled my hand away, I felt his strength become part of me—all ten feet and eight-hundred pounds of muscle, claws, and teeth.

"Thank you, brother tiger. May your strength serve me well in the war to come. No hard feelings."

I quickly left the animal and silently returned to the shuttlecraft I came in.

That night, I acquired the strength and skills of ten other animals from around the world. When I finally returned to the base, I was so tired that I fell into my bed and went straight to sleep. My dreams were filled with a faceless voice, always saying the same thing: "You must make a choice between vengeance and something more."

The next morning, I woke feeling tense, like something was going to happen soon. I spent the morning looking over the photo albums that took up three shelves in one of my bookcases, some of them containing old-fashioned human photos and some holographic Centaurien versions.

I looked up at the objects Terra and I had used to decorate our walls. We'd gone with a kind of war and peace theme, collecting artifacts from the past and around the world.

I looked at each sword and the bows I'd wielded until the human race invented gun powder. I also looked at the symbols of peace we'd added among them. Over the past five thousand years, I've learned to see the balance in history.

My eyes traveled to the mantel piece and the katana on an antler sword stand. Very slowly, I climbed to my feet and lifted it from the stand, handling the sword as if it were made of glass. I cradled it before twisting it around, grasping the handle, and slowly drew the sword from its sheath.

As I examined the blade, Damon entered and leaned against the doorframe. "I remember when you got that from your old father-in-law. What was his name again?" He stepped closer.

"Miyamoto Musashi," I said, returning the sword to the sheath.

"Yeah, I remember him. Damn, he was old." He smiled as he sat down.

I chuckled and leaned against the mantle. "Damon, you and I are old. He was young."

He nodded. "I guess you have a point." I picked up the albums and returned them to the shelf. "Ian, some of our people have been talking. Maybe we should modify—"

"As I already told Jen, we don't have a choice in this matter," I interrupted before he could say more. "Besides, there's something about these kids," I said, looking at a portrait of George Washington. "I think they may be the solution."

"They're just kids, Ian, and human. We all know most human actions lead to some form of destruction."

I turned and looked at him. "Were Centauriens any different, Damon?"

He opened and closed his mouth before he gave up.

I smiled. "Humans are a young race, but we've seen them grow. We've witnessed their capacity for good, and their courage is unlike anything we have seen in any race, including Centauriens and Paradines. "We've lived on this planet for five-thousand years; we know that, nine times out of ten, humans choose to do the right thing," I said.

He nodded. "I know, Ian, but this task is too big for these kids."

"You may be right, my friend, but I don't think so."

He sighed, stood, and headed for the door. "Their school gets out in half an hour. Maybe you should meet them."

After watching him go, I returned the sheathed sword to the mantle and placed my palms together, I bowing to it. I then went to the hangar and hopped on my bike. When I was off the base, I bought a slice for a late lunch and drove to Golden Dragon.

CHAPTER 17

THE HUNT

Alec

Hunter had managed to slip the tracking device into Bradley's backpack early the next morning. A few days later, as we looked at the data on the holographic readout, Pythia remarked, "Apart from going by the lake a few times when he was supposed to be in a bonfire beach party at Black Tiger, he hasn't done anything unusual."

"Nothing?" I asked, running my fingers down my cheek.

"Nothing." She turned her chair toward me.

I looked back to the holographic map of the lake. "Maybe that's the answer…"

"What is?" Blair asked, confused.

"The lake. What if they're in the lake?"

"What do you mean?" Pythia asked.

"The Wraiths must have a base nearby. What if they're *in* the lake?" I jabbed a finger at the hologram.

They looked at the map, faces brightening with the possibility. "Why *in* the lake, though?" Blair asked. "It has a couple dozen islands."

"People live on more than half of them," Hunter told her. "Someone would have noticed if the Wraiths were on an island."

Abruptly, Pythia moved to the computer and her fingers started flying.

"What are you doing?" Gavin moved closer.

"Just checking the lake's water level records," she answered without looking up.

"Find anything?" I asked.

"Record flooding two years ago, after a small storm," she answered. "Perhaps something large landed in it."

Filled with success, we grinned at each other. "Looks like we found them," Blair said. "The question is how do we get to them? I think they're going to notice if we scour the lake."

Pythia rolled over to a table holding an empty fish tank. "You wanted me to work on the stealth mode. I think I have the answer."

We looked into the tank and saw several houseflies, mosquitoes, and cockroaches moving about.

"Bugs?" Blair asked, surprised. "What do bugs have to do with it?"

Pythia said, "Remember when I told you the suits acquire the DNA of living organisms?" We nodded and she waved her hand at the insects.

"Don't you think people would notice giant... bugs?" Aisha asked.

"Or something like Baxter Stockman?" Hunter joined in.

Sighing, Pythia gave us a sideways look. "Do you also remember the suits can change your size to match the creature's DNA you acquire?"

I blinked, taken aback. "I thought you were joking," I said, stunned. "Have you tested that feature?" I looked at the bugs, feeling nervous.

"Would I have suggested it otherwise?"

CHAPTER 18

HELL

Ian

The next day at Golden Dragon, I was once more in the private class-room with Tora, training the teens. As we taught Aisha the round-house kick against one of the bags, I eyed Blair as she worked with another instructor.

She first threw an elbow to his gut. Mimicking the reaction, he bent over; after receiving a back fist to the face, she grabbed his head. Rolling forward, off her chair, she threw him to the mat, where she began to pound him.

Talk about blood thirsty, I thought and spied Alec as he got a drink from a bubbler in the corner. "Tora, take over," I said, and she nodded as I walked over to Alec. "Is everything okay?" I asked when I reach him.

Looking at me, he nodded. "Yeah, just thirsty."

I looked back at the others. "It's good to have you join us here at Golden Dragon," I said.

"It's good to be here," he said and took another sip.

After couple seconds I added, "They look up to you." He paused, looking at me. "Do you know the difference between a good leader and great one?" After a second, he shook his head. "The ones who follow you do it without being ordered," I answered, and he lowered his gaze in thought. "Come on," I said patting his shoulder, "let's get back to work."

After class, I watched the parents pick up the teens and then pulled out of the parking lot on my bike. For hours, I drove aimlessly around town, ignoring my ringing comm. Eventually, I stopped at the cliffs overlooking the ocean and killed the engine and climbed off. After walking to the edge, I sat on the rocks.

I inhaled the sea air, smiling as I remembered all the times Terra and I had come here. She'd always had a passion for the lakes and oceans of this planet. For a while, I just sat there, looking out at the water, but at the sound of an engine behind me, I turned my head.

Soon Jen, Casey, Jules, Damon, and Klaus were sitting on either side of me. "You didn't answer your comm link," Jules said.

"I wanted to be left alone," I replied as the sun started setting.

"What's going on, Ian? We're your friends. Of all people, we deserve to know," Jen said.

"Oh, come on, honey," Casey said sarcastically. "He's on such a good streak as it is." He settled his arm around her, and she grasped his hand.

"The two humans I captured told us where one of their operations might be based," I said. "I'm going there tonight, and I'm going to attack it."

All eyes turned to me.

"You've got to be joking, bro!"

"Ian, that's crazy!"

"You could get killed!"

"We need you here!"

I closed my eyes, erasing the masterpiece of a sunset. "I'll try to come back to you all, but if I don't—"

"Ian, don't talk like that!"

"If I don't, do me proud, Casey, and you, too, Jules." They stared at me as I stood, climbed on my bike, and took off before they could say another word.

Alec

That night, while wearing our Cybersuits, we hid in the forest across the street from Black Tiger. We watched Bradley and a few others arrive at the school, several sporting gym bags; I was relieved to see Bradley had his backpack.

I eyed Gavin. "This is going to be weird," I murmured.

"Weirder than me watching you turn into a faceless copy of me?" he replied in a robotic voice.

Hunter patted Gavin on the shoulder and said, "It's probably going to be a mode we'll use often."

Gavin jabbed his thumb over his shoulder toward the small crater Hunter had created earlier. "From the looks of things, I'm going to have to give you flying lessons."

"Children, focus," Pythia snapped over the commlink, her face appearing in a corner. "We've got a job to do!"

I took a deep breath to steady my nerves and nodded. "She's right! Let's get it done!"

I focused and, at once, robotic insect limbs sprang from my sides as insect wings sprouted from my back. My torso quickly reshaped to form a fly's abdomen, and my hands and feet shifted into fly feet. The armor became the thorax and head, and I was forced down onto all sixes.

Around me, my friends were going through similar transformations, and I watched as Blair's helmet began to reshape into the head of a fly.

Suddenly, the screen in front of me broke into compounded images, the ones right in front of me offering a smaller version of what I'd seen before. Around it, similar rectangular screens looked in all directions. It was like I was at a security station, watching feedback from a hundred security cameras, each showing different angles but couldn't see more than a few feet in front of me. Sensor readings were still being displayed. To my amazement, I realized I was starting to shrink, but then it stopped as suddenly as it started.

"Well, that was freaky!" I said, stunned. "Why didn't it hurt?"

"The nanites the Cybersuit injected into your bloodstream dulled your pain receptors temporarily. Now, get moving—you have only one hour. Keep an eye on the timer because, when it runs out, the suit will automatically revert!" Pythia said.

"Right!" I exclaimed as the timer appeared and the countdown started. "Let's bring it!" With a buzz, the wings of our fly bodies fired, and we lifted off, heading for Black Tiger. "Everyone keep close," I said as we neared the road. "This is going to be the hard part. Gain altitude and watch out for anything that'll eat us!"

"Hey, look on the bright side," Hunter said, "at least it's not raining." We all groaned.

When we reached the other side of the road, Hunter homed in on the tracking signal from the device still in Bradley's backpack.

"Has anyone figured out how we'll follow them to wherever the heck they're going?" Blair asked, and silence followed.

"Doesn't anybody pay attention in biology class these days?" Pythia asked, exasperated. "The dragonfly commonly feeds on flies and mosquitoes and is considered the best flyer in the insect world as they can go straight up, down, left, right, and hover like a helicopter. Doesn't it stand to reason that their prey would be almost as good at flying? Use that to hide!"

"Mental note: pay more attention in biology," I observed. "You heard the lady—once we're near the group, spread out and find a place to hide! Remember that we can move like helicopters!"

I've got to remember to get a dragonfly mode, I thought as the students came into our line of sight.

Ian

I crouched down in my Cybersuit from a position at the forest's edge and watched the group climb onto the boat. All had the same shimmering aura I'd noticed around the sensei at Black Tiger.

"It must be dinnertime," I said as I watched the boat leave the dock.

Softly and quietly, I slipped into the water until I was completely submerged, barely making a ripple. In the shape of a common lake trout, I followed the boat into deeper water.

Damn, I thought as a pair of jet drives popped out of my sides,

Shurgal wasn't kidding when he said the Cybersuit could enhance the acquired abilities. I slipped under the boat through the propeller wash to avoid being detected by a fish finder.

Alec

Hidden safely under the controls of the boat, we waited, feeling the vibrations of the motor through the Cybersuits.

"If this keeps up, I'm going to hurl!" Hunter moaned. "Pythia, you've got to improve the shocks on these things!"

"I'll look into that when you get back," she replied through the comms.

Suddenly, a new sound met our ears, and Aisha asked, "What the heck is that?"

"I'll have a look," I said. Before any of them could object, I flew forward and peeked over the edge of the controls. What I saw nearly made me fall to the floor. "You guys are not going to believe this," I said, stunned at the water rushing above us, "but I think this boat just turned into a submarine."

Ian

After the boat submerged, a force field over the top to keep the water out, I kept my distance.

After two minutes, I started to wonder how much longer this would take. Out of the darkness, a shape emerged, and I stopped dead at the sight of a ship.

"I found them," I reported. "Mark these quadrants."

"Done, Ian," Jen replied.

As I drew close to the ship, I grew in size and transformed. My tail fins split, forming legs with flipper-like feet, and ny hands were webbed. The fish head slipped down across my chest, revealing my Cybersuit face as I straightened the dorsal fin on top of my head like a mohawk.

I moved along the side of the ship and paused when I encountered an airlock. "Let's see if this suit can override this as easily as it hacked into El Dorado's communications," I murmured, resting a hand on the access port.

Almost at once, the door opened, and as water was sucked in, I was pulled inside. The airlock closed behind me, and as the water level began to drop, I focused and shifted back to normal Cybersuit mode.

Alec

We felt the submarine stopping, and together we climbed toward the edge to watch the possessed people exit. "Time for us to go," I said, and we all fired our wings and flipped over the edge to follow.

"Now what?" Aisha asked.

"We find a place to change back," I said, "and we do our best not to be seen."

"Oh yeah, the Wraiths surely won't notice a few Cybersuits walking around," Hunter said sarcastically.

"If you can each touch a Zorvain you will gain their camouflage ability," Pythia said through the comms.

"Then let's land on one and get what we need," Blair said.

"It doesn't work that way," Gavin's mom explained. "You can only acquire DNA in the normal Cybersuit mode."

If we'd had necks, we would have looked at each other. "Any ideas?" I asked.

"Well, the obvious solution is that one of us turns back and takes a Zorvain form," Blair said.

Before Pythia could reply, Aisha asked, "Do you hear that?"

Flying up, we landed upside-down on the ceiling and listened. After a moment, I heard screams.

"No! No, not again! Please! Someone help me! No!"

The desperate screams sent a chill down my spine.

"Allah be merciful," Aisha murmured. "I think we just entered hell."

CHAPTER 19

THE ENEMY

Alec

We moved toward the sound of the screams and found ourselves in a large, open area with a pulsing light in the center. We attached to the closest surface.

"Talk about being a fly on a wall!" Hunter murmured, and I was grateful to listen to something other than those blood-curdling screams.

"Pythia, is there a way to focus in on one of these compound views?" I asked, hoping I was just imagining what I could see on the screens.

"Stare at the screen you want," Pythia answered uneasily.

"Can you see and hear everything we can?" Gavin asked.

"Yes. Don't spare me, though."

Closing my eyes, I focused. When I opened them again, I stared in horror.

Hordes of people milled about in the area below. Many were races I couldn't even hope to identify, but most were human with legions of Zorvains and Sloozes. Taken aback by their number, I almost missed what was right below us.

A mist pulsed a strange light that swirled in on itself, forming a tight ball. Every now and then, I saw something shift within it, like an object caught inside a twister.

What really caught my attention, however, was the line of people in front of it. I watched as a well-dressed woman stepped toward the swirling mist and her face and form became indistinct, as if I were looking at her through a foggy glass. Her back arched, her arms spreading wide.

"By Allah, what is happening to her?" Aisha asked.

"No," Blair's voice weakly piped in. "Please, God, no."

In a huge exhalation, a gassy cloud separated from her body and seamlessly melded into the mist. From what Pythia had taught us, I was sure this was a Wraith.

As it disappeared, the woman jerked back. "Let me go! You can't keep doing this—I'm not a slave! Let me go!" she screamed as a small wall shot up behind her, then, and metal tentacles snapped around her wrists, securing her to it.

"Help! Oh, please, someone help! Help us all!" She continued to scream as she struggled against her bindings. She was lifted over the line of people by the small slab she was bound to.

As we followed its course, we saw what had to be the holding cell: a cut-out section of the wall where the Wraiths kept other free humans, Zorvains, and other races. Whenever one of the captives approached the edge, there was a flash of light and they leaped back in pain.

The slab of metal holding the well-dressed woman flew to an indentation in the wall before flipping around and depositing with the others, locking her in. There, her voice joined countless other pleas for help.

On the other side, of where the freed hosts were being kept, I watched as another set of tentacles shot out and snatched a man right off the ground where he sat, quickly followed by a young girl with curly, brown hair. We watched as these people, either struggling or hanging limply from their bindings, were carried before the mist. When they were in position, Wraiths rose from the mist, shifting through the air like water and melding with the captured people before them.

The bindings locked them in place as the Wraiths made contact. The victims' backs arched, horror on their faces, before they went calm and straight, their bindings retracting into the pillar which lowered into the floor. The people walked away, once more a prisoner in their own body.

"How are we supposed to stop this?" Hunter asked as we watched more suffer the same fate. "This is the dry cleaners from hell! How can five teens stop something like this?"

"Like this!" Blair shouted, and then she grew larger and larger.

CHAPTER 20

FIRST BLOOD

Alec

As Blair grew, she resumed the original form of the Cybersuit and then dropped to the ramp below, landing on one knee with loud *clang*.

All sound and movement stopped as she slowly rose to face them, and then the Zorvains charged her.

"I guess we follow her lead," I yelled, "but remind me to kill her later!"

As we each shifted back to Cybersuit mode and joined Blair, a restraining slate rose. Before the tentacles could shoot out and restrain us, my right forearm shifted, releasing the energy sword.

Twisting around, I sliced the panel near its base and fired a turning side kick, impacting the panel before it hit the ground. The force of the kick shot it toward the horde, knocking down people and squishing two Zorvains against the opposite wall.

"Now!" I shouted, and we all leaped forward.

I landed on top of two more Zorvains and cut one in half with one great slash of the sword. My other forearm converted into a sonic stun cannon, and I spun around and fired, sending a line of people tumbling through the air.

Beside me, Hunter lifted a man over his head with one hand while he kicked another, and then he tossed him at a third man and a woman, knocking them to the deck.

Behind him, Blair reminded me of a cowgirl in an old-fashioned western shootout as both her cannons blazed. At her back, Aisha covered her with an energy sword and an object that looked like a blend of a sledgehammer and a mace.

Nearby, Gavin was having trouble. He wielded a pair of sticks with sharp tips, but his massive wings hindered his movement in close quarters. I shoved a woman aside and decapitated a Zorvain, and then I jumped to drop down on a Zorvain coming toward Gavin from behind. I fired the sonic cannon again, sending a few more bodies flying, and Gavin nodded in thanks.

As I turned my forearm to retract the sonic cannon and delivered a powerful punch that sent a man to the ground, I heard a sound rise above the shouts and cannon fire: cheering.

I glanced around to find the source, and my eyes fell on the people in the holding area. They gathered around the force field, some were brandishing fists but all cheering us on.

"Aisha! Blair!" I said into the commlink. "The repossession line!"

"We're on it!" Blair replied, and the pair hurried toward the people bound to restraining slabs. Aisha sliced the planks from their bases and cut the captives free.

"Gavin! Hunter! The holding cell!"

"On it!" Gavin called, bringing his wings forward, the feathers pointed at the consoles. Two metal feathers fired, imbedding themselves in the console before it exploded. The force field died with a flicker of light, and the people poured out.

"Keep together, and let's get the heck out of here!" Hunter called as he started leading them out of the cell.

Just then, something slammed me hard in the back, knocking me down, and an alarm sounded as the armor covering my back flashed on the readout.

"Alec, what happened?" Pythia demanded as I rolled over. "The armor on your back just took a serious hit!"

Before I could answer, a Zorvain appeared in my line of vision, pointing a blaster at my face.

"Hey!" This shout came from an unfamiliar altered voice, and the Zorvain looked up as rapid-fire blaster rounds jerked its body.

The figure who saved me stood in a hatch, arm raised. Although it wore a Cybersuit, it looked different. The muscular body was black from head to toe, with a spot or rosette pattern I could barely see. It stood on two paw-like feet with high-arched heels, and a tail swished behind it. The armored hands were also paw-like, and on the side of its head, two cat-like ears rose to sharp points.

One arm pointed in my direction, and a pair raised slot on its forearm one near where the wrist met the hand and the other higher up near the elbow. Each with a pair of barrels mounted under them. I watched as the slots lowered seamlessly back into place like they had never been there.

Crouching, it leaped toward me, legs tucked in, and when it landed next to me, I saw a flash as three-inch claws appeared from the tips of its fingers. It slashed one paw at a Zorvain, and a set of claw slashes appeared across its throat.

Turning to me, it offered a hand and helped me up. "You're either incredibly brave or incredibly stupid," it said to me, and I realized the altered voice sounded male. Abruptly, he shoved me aside and kicked a man coming up behind me. I watched, amazed, as he delivered a few more side kicks, knocking more Zorvains away.

We moved back to the others, and everyone headed toward the hatch. It opened suddenly, revealing another figure in a Cybersuit. Beside me, the cat-like figure said, "Kizor!"

CHAPTER 21

SAVE AS MANY AS YOU CAN

Ian

With my blood boiling with rage, I moved to the front of the group.

Kizor's shoulders shook and he chuckled. "I must say this is indeed a surprise. Now I won't have to hunt you down."

"What makes you think we're not getting out of here?" I demanded, shifting my stance and activating my claws.

"You have enemies both in front and behind," Kizor observed.

Frowning, I sent a quick glance behind me. None of the teens had taken a rear-guard position, and now the freed people and Zorvains inched back as they were closed in on by those still possessed.

"It is time for you all to die!" Kizor expanded, becoming large and round. His head and limbs disappeared into his torso, which continued to balloon until he almost filled the corridor.

I isolated the commlink frequency the teens were communicating on so we couldn't be overheard and looked at the hatches on either side. "Can you hear me?"

They flinched. One of them said, "How—"

"Not now!" I barked. "If he's becoming what I think he's becoming, we need to run now! He's about to lose his vision and then get it back tenfold! Save as many as you can! Understood?"

Another one started, "But how—"

"Understood?" I snapped again.

"Yeah, we got it," a third one said.

"On my signal," I told them, shifting back again as Kizor's face disappeared into his body. "Now!"

Three to a group, we shepherded the freed hosts toward the closed hatches as fast as we could. We didn't get far before circular blobs appeared at the top of Kizor's body. Squid-like tentacles then shot out of what he had become and seized four of the fleeing people.

As those who remained with us barreled through the hatches, I watched in horror as Kizor opened a gaping mouth full of teeth like a meat grinder and shoveled the screaming people inside with his tentacles. My vision turned to x-ray mode, and I sighed when I saw the people fall through Kizor's mouth into some kind of container where his stomach should have been.

At least they're alive, I thought as I jumped through the hatch, *but after he releases them for repossession, they're going to wish he'd killed them.* When the hatch sealed behind me, I slashed the controls with my claws, the circuits sparking.

Alec

With the big cat guy right behind me, my friends and I rushed down the hall as fast as we could. When we reached an intersection, I skidded to a stop, trying to figure out where to go next.

"No, wait!" the man said, and I pivoted and saw he was back in normal Cybersuit mode. He turned his head rapidly to look down each hall.

"Why do those things have to be so hard to detect?" he muttered.

"What are you—"

Before I could finish my question, four tentacles snapped out of nowhere, snatching people down the hall right off their feet. I whipped around just in time to see the creature called Kizor swallow them.

"Take half that way," the Cybersuited man told Blair and Aisha. "We'll go this way!"

They took off just as Kizor came at us at high speed, his enormous, blob of a figure rolling quickly across the deck.

I stopped, my feet digging in, and stepped in front of its path as it came at me. My forearm shifted into a cannon, and I lifted my arm and held it steady with my opposite hand as it hummed with a charge and targeted Kizor.

"No, don't!" the man snapped at me just as I fired.

The blast hit it dead center, and Kizor didn't even try to dodge. He exploded, breaking up into four separate parts. As I lowered my arm, I saw that the people he'd swallowed, contained in some kind of membrane, were still alive as they beat their fists against the transparent film.

Before I could charge forward to free them, I froze in horror. Like a starfish, the four separate parts rapidly became four identical but smaller versions of the original creature. They all faced us, and suddenly, each one shot forward, snatching people as it went and growing larger with each recapture.

Before I could move, the Cybersuited man grabbed me from behind and dragged me into a corridor. When he released me, he pressed a button on the wall and the door slammed closed.

"You just gave him a way to hunt us all down!" he snapped, glaring at me before he punched through the door controls. He shifted into the form of a large white tiger with stand out black stripes and yelled, "We don't have much time!"

Ian

We had reached an airlock with the riders still on my back. After trans¬forming again to a similar battle mode—this one more muscled and with more tiger like features around my face, I opened the airlock and we started to pile in.

I paused at the sound of pounding, clawed feet.

"They're going to be on us before we can equalize the lock," one of the men said, turning to look at me.

After a pained look, he shoved the other man in. He looked at me before he sealed the door in my face just as I leaped forward to stop him. He looked at us through the force field and pressed his hand against it.

Pressing my hand to his, we looked at each other. "None of us will forget this, and you will be free—I swear it," I pledged. He nodded in return and then darted toward the sound of the feet.

After starting the equalizing process, I moved toward the inner door to watch him stand alone against the oncoming Wraiths. The other two Cybersuited teens moved next to me.

"Stand aside!" a young voice said as the Cybersuit next to me stiffened.

"You'll have to kill me first!" the man growled, bending his knees and raising his fists.

The voice laughed, "Do we?"

Two Zorvains appeared on either side of him, seized his upper arms, and tossed him aside like an old shoe.

As the Zorvains moved, I saw a small girl behind them with brown hair that stretched down to her shoulders. She stood in front of a line of armed, possessed Zorvains and humans.

"No!" the Cybersuit next to me screamed as he pounded against the inner door.

"Stop!" I shouted, and the other teen and I grabbed him and pulled him back. "If you damage that door, you could decompress the whole ship! Do you understand what that means?"

"I don't care—I have to get to her!" He then froze like his Cybersuit had been paralyzed.

Releasing him, I quickly shifted to a fish and then into battle mode. "We're leaving now!" I shouted as the water reached the ceiling and the outer door opened.

I grabbed the human and the unmoving suited figure; his friend grabbed his ankle before we shot out of the airlock and into the lake at an astonishing speed. Glancing back, I could just make out the little girl's face, which bore a look of pure hatred.

CHAPTER 22
BAND OF BROTHERS AND SISTERS

Ian

When we made it to the shore of the lake, I shifted to my normal Cybersuit and then turned and stopped the other teen from dragging his friend.

"We need to get out of here!" he snapped.

"Yeah, and I'd rather not leave a trail of bread crumbs!" I retorted. "Can whoever paralyzed this kid's suit hear me?" I asked privately.

"Yes," a female voice finally said.

"Turn the suit back on—we need to get moving again!"

After a long pause, the teen suddenly dashed back toward the lake; I grabbed him just before he reached the water and pinned him to the ground.

"I don't know what your problem is," I growled, "but if we don't leave now, the Wraiths will find us, the human we saved will be repossessed, and the rest of us could be killed!" He continued to struggle, so I added, "If you keep this up, I'll have the person on the comms paralyze you again or take control! Do you understand me?" For a second, he remained silent. "Do you understand?"

"Yeah!" he snarled at last and climbed to his feet.

I turned to the other Cybersuit. "Is there a place you're supposed to meet the others if you get separated?"

"Yes, this way." He turned into the forest.

I tossed the newly freed man over my shoulder and followed him, making sure the other teen stayed behind me. When we came to a stop, I set the man back on his feet. He took several steps back, studying us, as I scanned the area for the other three teenagers.

"Oh God, please let them be okay," the one I'd pinned down moaned.

"Where's your faith?" I turned and watched as the other teens walked out of the trees with a human woman behind them.

My forearm shifted into the omega cannon, and the right view mode came up. The woman didn't have a shimmering aura, and as far as I could tell, the same was true for the other three. *But can the view penetrate their suits?* I wondered.

They came toward us, and the teens exchanged handshakes and hugs.

I stepped forward and asked, "How did you get away from Kizor?"

"Who?" one of the girls said.

The other girl chimed in, "The psycho in octopus-from-hell form?"

"That would be him," I replied. "How did you escape?"

"Let's just say we managed to touch the right animal to gain the right mode," one said, "and then persuaded him to reconsider." They held up a section of sliced tentacle.

"Not bad," I said, my forearm shifting back, "but now it's time for a serious talk, like we should have had after I dropped that chair off at your school."

"That was you?" I guessed it was Blair who asked and marked her with a name.

"Yes, and I have a lot to say. First, all of you made mistakes tonight that nearly got you killed! Worse, those mistakes could have destroyed the Cybersuits or allowed them to be captured, and we cannot let them fall into enemy hands!"

They stared at the ground as I kept an eye on the two humans we'd managed to free this night. "You were all really lucky, and I suggest you end on that note. Walk away from this life—especially if you're going to be reckless!"

"Not going to happen!"

I looked at the one I had dragged from the lake. "What happens the next time you're up against them?" I demanded. "What if one you gets killed? Can you live with that? You don't belong to the war you stumbled into."

"I don't care if we failed tonight!" the boy shouted. "I don't know about my friends, but I'm going to keep going until either we win or I'm dead!" I froze at the conviction in his tone. "That little girl down there is my sister!"

"What?"

"Are you sure it was her?"

I froze, and memories of Johanna flashed through my mind, as well as all my fears of what had happened to her. As I slowly faced him, I could feel his hatred and anger, even though the suit.

"Maybe if the Wraiths had taken *your* family, you'd understand," he said.

I kept my temper in check as I faced him fully and held the gaze I felt from his blank, metal face.

"Very well," I said simply. "Tonight wasn't a defeat but your first and possibly greatest victory."

"How?" the winged Paradine challenged. "We barely got out of there alive!"

"Exactly," and we looked over as rivers of tears of happiness ran down the freed woman's face. "Now everyone they've enslaved knows there's someone out here fighting for them, and that will give them something the Wraiths have been trying to stamp out since day one: hope."

Nodding I looked at the teens. "Now, I suggest you get out of here before they send people to look for us."

"What about you?"

"I'll see you around," I answered, shifting into Paradine mode before darting forward and grabbing the two humans. "Hold on!" I barked to them, and we soared into the night.

When we arrived at the base, my friends and family greeted me with hugs, grateful that I had survived.

I looked at the two humans as they looked around them. "I assure you that you are safe here," I said before stepping out of the Cybersuit.

"What are you people?" the man asked.

"We're free Centauriens, and this is our base here on Earth. We'll have to debrief you later, but until then, you can stay in the quarters we'll assign you."

Jules came forward and signaled to a pair of men in uniform, who came forward and led them away.

I described the events in the Wraith ship, and my friends and family were amazed at what the teens had achieved. I then excused myself and headed for one of the hallways.

After stopping in front of a pair of thick metal doors, I entered a code into the holographic keypad. The doors hissed open, and I stepped inside to see bare walls and no other doors. I soon came to a dead end.

"Good evening, Ann," I said.

A moment later, the wall in front of me vanished and the force field deactivated. In front of me, a woman behind a desk operated a computer, a holo screen floating in front of her. Off to the side was a counter holding a retinal, hand, voice, and DNA scanner.

"Sir, please step up to the identification panel," she commanded.

I did as I was told and placed my hand on the pad. I then bent to rest my upper face against the frame of the retinal and eye scanner. "Dregan, Ian, Commander, 007 Alpha Tango 481," I said. The tip of one of my fingers began to sting.

After a moment, the computer authorized me to proceed, and a key card slid out. I pulled it out and went to Ann, who kept a hand under the desk and her eyes on me as I slid the key card into a slot on the wall. There was a *beep* before part of the wall slid inward and to the side. I stepped up to the opening, inhaled, and stepped through. Nothing happened.

I turned to look at Ann, and she finally relaxed and took her hand off her blaster.

"Let me know when you're finished, sir," she said.

The door closed behind me, and I was sealed in. I turned to the computer in the room—the only computer that held all of our new codes and changed them regularly. It secured information on our forces, including a list of Centauriens living in the human world, as well as our allies. I pressed a button and a chair unfolded from under the desk. When I sat down, I powered up the holo desktop.

After I selected the program I wanted, I quickly typed in the names *Alec, Hunter, Blair,* and *Aisha*, creating a new file in our forces. I finished by adding my name to it. The program asked for a code name, and after a moment of thought, I typed ten letters: W-I-L-D H-E-A-R-T-S.

For he today that sheds his blood with me, shall be my brother.

~ William Shakespeare

Made in the USA
Middletown, DE
24 July 2018